Hugo Erichsen, Willis Percival King

**Medical rhymes**

A collection of rhymes of the anciente time and rhymes of the modern day

Hugo Erichsen, Willis Percival King

**Medical rhymes**
*A collection of rhymes of the anciente time and rhymes of the modern day*

ISBN/EAN: 9783337274115

Printed in Europe, USA, Canada, Australia, Japan

Cover: Foto ©Andreas Hilbeck / pixelio.de

More available books at **www.hansebooks.com**

"Acestes next
His arrow towards the heavens straightway directs.
It speeds its way athwart the liquid clouds,
When, lo! a trail of fire its path enshrouds."

# MEDICAL RHYMES.

—A COLLECTION OF—

Rhymes of ye Ancients Time, and Rhymes of the Modern
Day; Rhymes Grave and Rhymes Mirthful; Rhymes
Anatomical, Therapeutical and Surgical; all
Sorts of Rhymes to Interest, Amuse
and Edify all Sorts of Fol-
lowers of Esculapius.

## SELECTED AND COMPILED FROM A VARIETY OF SOURCES,

—BY—

## HUGO ERICHSEN, M. D.,

*Professor of Neurology in the Quincy School of Medicine, Medical Department of
Chaddock College; Licentiate of the Royal College of Physicians and Surgeons
of Kingston, Canada; Member of the Detroit Medical and Library
Association; Corresponding Member of the Natural
History Society of Wisconsin, etc.*

—WITH AN—

## INTRODUCTION

—BY—

## PROF. WILLIS P. KING, M. D., Sedalia, Mo.

*Ex-President of Missouri State Medical Society, etc.*

---

## ILLUSTRATED

---

## J. H. CHAMBERS & CO.,

St. Louis, Mo.,          Chicago, Ill.          Atlanta, Ga.

1884.

# PREFACE.

Compilations of medical poems have been issued in France by Dr. G. J. Witkowski and in Germany by Dr. Ludwig Heymann and others. In the English tongue none has heretofore appeared, and this must be looked upon as a novelty. The purpose of my book is to amuse the busy doctor in leisure hours. Some of the serious poems will no doubt furnish food for reflection.

I hope the profession will read this book with pleasure. I wish most sincerely to thank those gentlemen who have aided me in the preparation of this book, and without whose kind help the work would not have been completed.

I must also acknowledge my indebtedness to Messrs. Houghton, Mifflin & Co., of Boston, Mass., for being allowed to reprint some of the copyrighted poems of Dr. O. W. Holmes.

H. E.

Detroit, Mich.

# INTRODUCTION.

THAT a doctor should write poetry at any time or under any circumstances may be a matter of surprise, and it, perhaps, surprises nobody more than the doctor himself.

A doctor with ability in any direction beyond that of being able to pour beans into a rat-hole is in a continual state of suppression. This arises not from any desire upon the part of the doctor to be *suppressed*. Oh, no! Doctors are human beings, and would enjoy all the liberty and latitude that is given other human beings. But his suppression is the result of a sort of public demand that a doctor shall be a doctor and nothing else.

People, in general, have very peculiar ideas about doctors. One is that a man whom they have known before he became a doctor cannot be a doctor. In other words—the doctors whom they know and recognize as such, *have been doctors ever since they knew them.* Hence the great difficulty of a young graduate obtaining practice in the neighborhood or town where he was born and raised. I have often heard the expression, "Why, he is no doctor. I have known Jim So-and-so ever since he was born;" and howsoever well educated Jim So-and-so may be, and howsoever well qualified he may be for the practice of his profession, the merest dummy, *whom the people know as Dr. Dummy the first time they meet him,* will take the bread and butter right out of his mouth. The "snorting populace" does not stop to consider that Dr. Dummy had to begin with anatomy and go through the regular course, just as Jim So-and-so had to do, the difference being that they can be tolerable certain as to the advantages that poor Jim has had and not so certain as to the advantages, qualifications and honesty of Dr. Dummy.

Another popular idea is that the doctor must practice medicine and do nothing else. Indeed, it is dangerous for him to *seem* to have qualifications for anything else. Has the doctor a good tenor voice and an ear for music, and does his soul yearn at times to join the church choir or to sing with the quartette at the charity sociable? Let him try it! Mrs. Grundy will level her spectacles and metaphorically wither him with the contempt that she will fling into her gaze. "Well, if there ain't Dr. Harmony a-singin' like a fool! and it ain't a week since I was a-takin' out of his pison. I thought then there was somethin' wrong, and now I know what it is; he's one of them fool singers."

Dr. Harmony's "*hash* is settled" with Mrs. Grundy ever thereafter.

Has the doctor aspirations in a political way? Let him "come out and declare himself" for some office; or, let him make a speech at a political meeting. That will settle him. They say he is "dabbling in politics, and not thinking about sickness," as if the doctor must forever go about with his head bowed down in deep contemplation of the details of the last cholera epidemic, or "figuring" on the size and propagating qualifications of the *bacillus tuberculosis*.

An old lady said to the writer once: "Now, doctor, I don't want you to go off down town and go to talkin' and crackin' jokes with the men folks. I want you to put in your time to-day a thinkin' about my liver." I knew all about her liver then that I could possibly have known if I had secluded myself and "put in my time a-thinkin'" for a whole month.

The writer also remembers to have lost caste at one time by writing a little poem which got into his very soul and would not "down" until it was put into form and published. About the same time he "made a few remarks" at a temperance meeting, in which he treated both sides of the vexed question with great fairness—the speech being made in the midst of exciting times which finally culminated in a riot—and he remembers to have lost at least one thousand dollars in practice annually for the next three years. Indeed he is not certain that he is done losing on that speech yet. The speech has already cost him at the rate of two or three dollars for every word, and yet it was not, by any means "the greatest effort of his life."

There are many more things required of a doctor by the exacting public which it is not necessary to enumerate or mention in this short introduction. I will mention one, however. It will be remembered by the reader that the old time "country doctor" always carried sweet spirits of nitre and creosote. These drugs smell very loud to one not continually in their vicinity. I can remember that I could smell our family physician almost as far as I could see him. He carried the nitre for the purpose of "cooling the fever" and the creosote for "morning sickness" in pregnant women, and for the toothache, of which last malady there was an abundance in the olden time before the advent of the dentist. When I began practice I went to the country. In one of my first cases I met an old woman with a sharp nose and a baleful glance, who looked me over and *through* and pretty thoroughly invoiced me. I learned a few days afterward that she had made the following comments on me after I had departed: "Well he looks like a doctor and *acts* a good deal like a doctor, but he don't *smell* a bit like one !" I knew what that meant, and so included sweet spirits of nitre and creosote in my next order for medicines. A doctor must not only refrain from many things which other mortals do, and which the promptings of his nature impel him to do, and do certain other things which make him feel like a fool, because he is acting "agin natur," but he must actually have a *professional* smell about him ! He is, perhaps, the only being in the broad universe, except the skunk and the billy-goat, whom people expect to recognize by his peculiar odor.

The bewildered but talented student who wrote the poem on "Par Vagum" perhaps exhibited it to his newly made friends where he first hung out his shingle and paid the penalty for his temerity by having to "seek greener fields and pastures new" within six months, and so with every other poem written by a doctor in this volume. Every line of them has cost the author of it its weight in diamonds.

And why should not the doctor write poetry, pray ? Is there not enough in his life's experience to make him a poet ? to make him loving, tender, sad, pathetic, satirical, passionate, gloomy and even suicidal ?

If he has the poetic temperament can he see the sad mother wailing over the loss of her only child and her first born without being moved in the innermost depths of his nature, and feeling like breaking out in pathetic rhyme ?

Can he stand by day after day and see the heroic struggle of wife, mother, father, son or daughter in grand efforts to save a loved one without feeling like crowning such devotion in immortal verse ?

There are a thousand and one things in the life of every doctor which are calculated to cause him to "break out" with violent attacks of rhyming. But he must not do it. He must walk with his head down, look as stupid as a donkey in a rainstorm, talk in monosyllables, think about people's livers, and be a *dummy* on all subjects that he may feel an interest in, excepting medicine; and, if he is a good deal of a *dummy* in that, and especially if he clothes himself with an air of profound mystery he will succeed the better with the great untutored mob. But, if he has talent, he is in a state of suppression, no matter what success may crown his acting against his strongest inclinations. "Then what can a doctor do?" He can practice medicine and that alone; practice patiently and toilfully from year to year. Wait for his pay until next year's crop is harvested and sold, and then do more work to get it than he did to earn it in the first place. He must be silent on politics and have no religion which conflicts with his patients' preconceived ideas of how he should mount the "golden stairs" through faith, repentance and baptism, or repentance, faith and baptism, as the case may be. He should prepare to be serious at all times; for hilarity in a doctor, it is held, belongs to the list of the "seven deadly sins." He may be snappish and crusty, if he wishes, for that is held to be an evidence of his great talent for business. He should also hold medicine as a great mystery, for the doctor who is weak enough to *explain* anything to a patient is supposed to know very little.

He must always be at home when he is wanted. The doctor who cannot be ubiquitous at all times is supposed not to attend to business. He is expected to attend to all of the charity practice in his bailiwick, for while the county court will refund to the merchant, the grocer and the citizens. goods, groceries and moneys furnished by them to the poor. the doctor may prepare to be *snubbed* if he presents his bill and asks a return from the public for services rendered the poor.

The doctor in order to rise in the world, must be slandered, traduced and lied about in all conceivable ways. Persons, who would not think of making anybody else a mark for slander and contemptuous remarks, will not hesitate to pick the neighborhood doctor to pieces for the benefit of the lolling crowd. In short the doctor is a patient public pack-horse, who is supposed to have acquired the ability to extract his living from the atmosphere, while he was preparing himself for a public sacrifice as a practi-

tioner of medicine.   He must do all the charity that comes in
his line without expectation of return, bear with all of the petty
annoyances of all the "nervous cranks" who fall under his care
and look for his pay "in the sweet by and by."

WILLIS P. KING.

Sedalia,  Mo.

# CONTENTS.

## ANATOMICAL LORE.

## FOR YE STUDENT MEN.

## THE DOCTOR HIMSELF.

## MEDICINE.

## SURGERY.

## OBSTETRICS.

## MISCELLANEOUS POEMS.

# ILLUSTRATIONS.

# INDEX.

# ANATOMICAL LORE.

## WITH THE SCALPEL.

### BY H. SAVILE CLARKE.

Here's our "subject," tall and strong,
　With vermilion well injected;
Where the blood once coursed along,
　Ready now to be dissected.
Some one never claimed, it seems,
　Friendless amid London's Babel:
Did he ever in his dreams
　　　See this table?

Here's a hand that once held fast
　All things pleasant, to its liking;
Now its active days are past,
　Or for friendship, or for striking.
Nothing colder here could lie,
　Yet on some one's palm there lingers
Sense of its warm touch, while I
　　　Strip the fingers.

How the dead eyes strangely stare,
　When I lift the lids above them!
Yet some woman lives, I swear,
　Who too well had learnt to love them;
Some one since their final sleep
　Holds their smiles in recollection.
While I put them by to keep
　　　For dissection.

Then the heart.   I take it out,
    Handling it with no compunction;
Once it wildly pulsed, no doubt,
    Well performed each wondrous function.

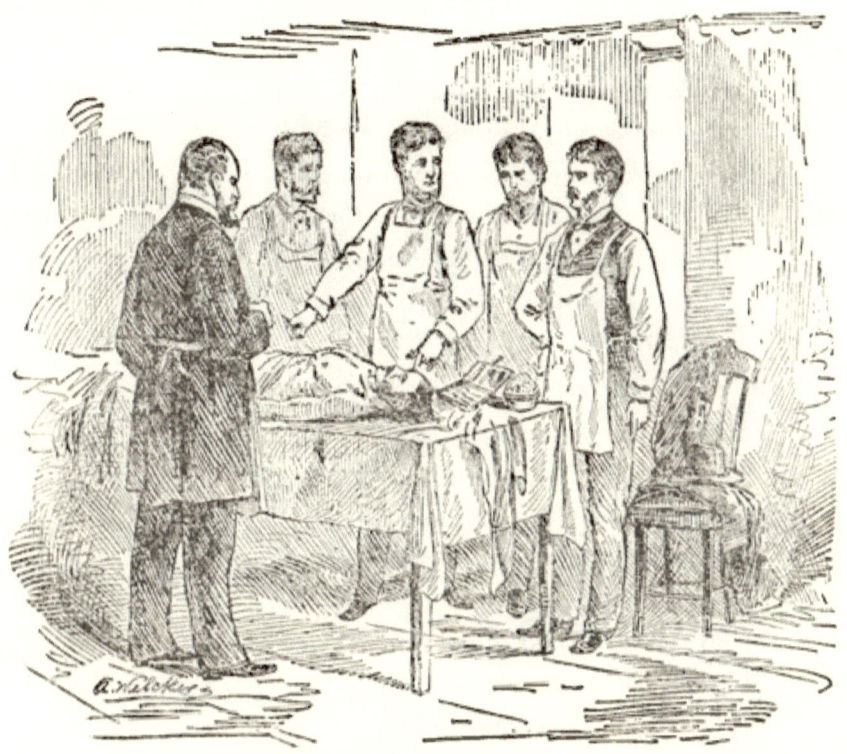

"Here's our 'subject,' tall and strong."

Sped the life-blood in its race
    In miraculous gyration,
Felt, responsive to one face,
        Palpitation.

Where was life then?   Was it hid
  In each curious convolution,
Packed beneath the cranium lid
  With such order'd distribution?
Can we touch one spot and say,
  Here all thought and feeling entered,
Here—'twas but the other day—
          Life was centred?

No, that puzzle still remains,
  One unsolved, supreme attraction;
Here are muscles, nerves and veins—
  Where was that which gave them action?
Though the scalpel's edge be keen,
  Comes no answer from the tissues,
Telling us where life has been —
          Whence it issues.

We can bid the heart be still,
  Stop the life-blood's circulation;
Paralyze the sovereign will,
  Through the centres of sensation,
When the clay lies at your feet,
  We can light no life within it,
Cannot make the dead heart beat
          For one minute.

Yet this thought remains with him,
  Dead he is to outward seeming,
Still the eyes, so glazed and dim,
  See what lies beyond our dreaming;
Know the secret of the spheres,
  Truth of doom or bliss supernal,
Read the riddle of the years—
          Life eternal!

So we'll leave him, ready now
   For to-morrow morning's lecture,
Little recks that placid brow
   Of our wayward wild conjecture.
It may be our fate to die
   All unwept and missed by no men —
As he lies there we may lie ;
       Absit omen.

---

## THE LARYNX TREE.

*A Poem Composed by a Student after Six Weeks Extra Quizzing.*

Par Vagum sits at his cottage door,
   Beneath the larynx tree,
And watches the biceps on the shore
   Sport with the diploë;
The umbilicus shows its blossoms red,
   To the sweet patella vine,
Which modestly droops its tender head,
   At the gaze of the santonine.

The astragalus rears its purple bloom,
   And the white trochanter flowers
Fill all the air with sweet perfume,
   Amid the splanchnic bowers.
No joy they bring to Par Vagum's heart,
   As, 'neath the larynx tree,
He brokenly leads a life apart,
   From his love far over the sea.

Sadly he thinks of the days now gone,
　Sweet and filled with bliss,
When the crowning joy of his life was one
　Angina pectoris.

Oh, Love's young dream was short and sweet,
　For Buccinator came,
And, kneeling at the false one's feet,
　Asked her to bear his name;
But she, as false as fair, was won,
　Oh, cruel, cruel sin !
By Buccinator's treacherous sire
　The artful Billi-Verdin.

Par Vagum fled his native shore,
　By the far-off carpal sea;
And there, by the antrum of Highmore
　His lonely home will be.
There, where no news of her may come,
　In his cot beside the sea,
He plays the light duodenum,
　Beneath the larynx tree.

Sad is his fate in that silent cot,
But death his pain will ease;
　And from his grave in that lonely spot
Will spring ascarides:
　And pilgrims of love, with tears will lave
His tomb 'neath the larynx tree,
　Writing this epitaph over his grave,
"Noli me tangere."

　　　　　　　　　—Medical Bulletin.

## SCIENCE AND LOVE.

Pray tell me my own dainty darling,
   About your centripetal nerve;
Is your cerebral ganglion working
   In a manner I like to observe?

Does the gray matter answer my pleading,
   And cause vaso-motors to move?
Ah, dearest, do let the medulla
   Oblongata respond to my love.

Your corpora quadrigemini, sweet one,
   As also the pons Varolii,
I love with an earnest affection,
   The result of complex stimuli.

And this co-ordination of atoms
   My cerebrum will still carry on,
Till cardiac motion be ended,
   And peripheral feeling be gone.

Then relax all your facial muscles,
   As the nerves of ambition vibrate:
Of your heterogeneous feelings
   Make a dear homogeneous state.

When the ganglia growing compounded,
   In the great bi-lobed mass effloresce,
Let them send through the thorax sensation
   To prompt an articulate "Yes!"

## LINES TO A SKELETON.

Sixty years ago the London Morning Chronicle published a poem enti-
tled, " Lines to a Skeleton," which excited much attention. Every effort,
even to the offering of fifty guineas, was vainly made to discover the
author. All that ever transpired was that the poem, in a fair clerkly
hand, was found near a skeleton of remarkable beauty of form and color,
in the museum of the Royal College of Surgeons, Lincoln's Inn, London.

Behold this ruin ! 'Twas a skull
Once of ethereal spirit full;
This narrow cell was life's retreat,
This space was Thought's mysterious seat.
What beauteous visions filled this spot !
What dreams of pleasure long forgot !
Nor hope nor pleasure, joy nor fear,
Has left one trace of record here.

Beneath this moldering canopy
Once shone the bright and busy eye;
But start not at the dismal void—
If social love that eye employed,
If with no lawless fire it gleamed,
But through the dews of kindness beamed,
That eye shall be forever bright,
When stars and suns are sunk in night.

Within this hollow cavern hung
The ready, swift and tuneful tongue:
If falsehood's honey it disdained,
And where it could not praise was chained,
If bold in virtue's cause it spoke,
Yet gentle concord never broke.
This silent tongue shall plead for thee
When time unveils eternity.

Say, did these fingers delve the mine,
Or with its envied rubies shine?
To hew the rock, or wear the gem
Can little now avail to them.

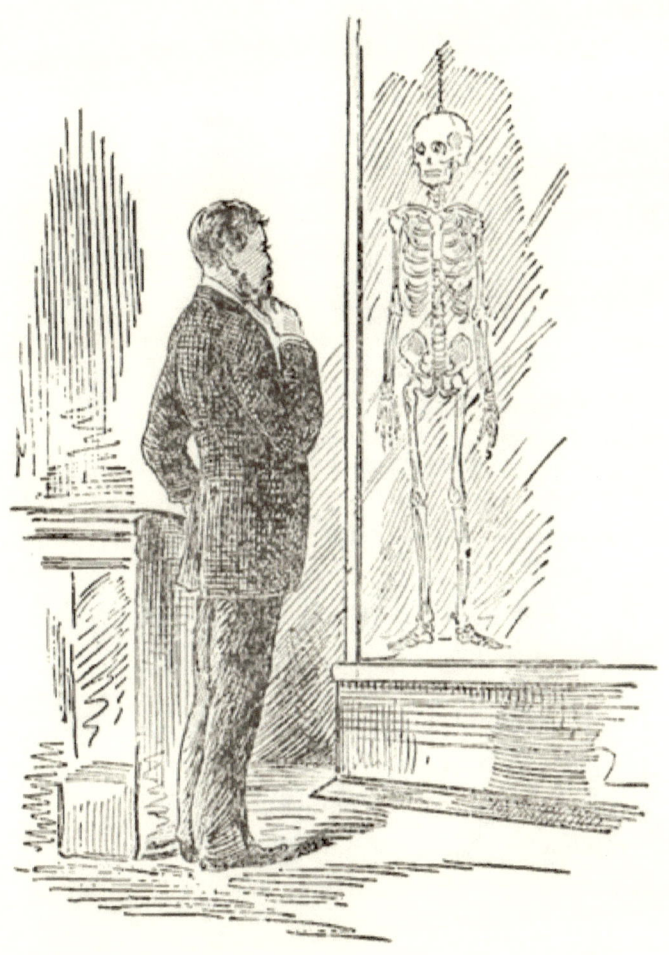

"Behold this ruin!"

But, if the path of truth they sought,
Or comfort to the mourner brought,

These hands a richer meed shall claim
Than all that wait on Wealth or Fame.

Avails it whether bare or shod
These feet the path of duty trod,
If from the bowers of ease they fled,
To seek Affliction's humble bed;
If Grandeur's guilty bribe they spurned,
And home to Virtue's cot returned,
These feet with angel's wings shall vie
And tread the palace of the sky.

## THE PRIME VIÆ.

BY DR. THOS. W. POOLE, LINDSAY, ONTARIO.

Primæ viæ,—Ductus vitæ,
Has e'er poet sung of thee;
Of thy rich digestive juices,
Acting all in harmony?

Duodenal glands of Brunner,
Rich as jewels in a shrine;
Follicles and crypts sub-mucal,
Grander far than palace ducal;
All the works of art outshine.

Epithelial cells, columnar,
Line thy arches far and wide:
Sentinels, on outpost duty,
Gems of protoplasmic beauty,
Laved by every passing tide.

Here the villi dip their noses ;
Gifted with a wond'rous power,
Not of smell, but of selection,
Of acceptance or rejection
Of the products of the hour.

Noble Villi !   Who instructs ye
Thus to choose our boon, or bane ?
How do ye secure your treasure ?
How transmit it at your leisure ?
Questions, yet to ask in vain.

Organs delicate, and moulded
On a microscopic plan,
Working transformations mighty,
Is it not the ductus vitæ,
After all, that makes the man ?

See that particle of butter,
Now an oil globe on its way !
The saliva lightly kissed it,
But the gastric juice has missed it,
And the purling stream has whisked it
In a duodenal bay.

There coquetting with a portion
Of the undigested rice,
The hepatic fluid meets them,
Pancreatic juices greet them,
And they're married in a trice.

Thus emulsionized and chylous,
Higher still the process goes;
Villus, lacteal, lymphatic,
Vital, chemical and static,
Till to bioplasm it grows,

Primæ viæ, ductus vitæ,
Half thy story is unsung;
Uncongenial much that passes,
Hydro-sulphurets and gases,
Fecal matters from thee wrung.

From the folds of deep mucosa
Creep a thousand tiny rills;
Bearing with them, as they issue,
Waste of nerve, debris of tissue,
Else the source of many ills.

Happy he whose daily promptings
Urge to defecation due,
Needing neither pills nor potions,
Regular as his devotions,
Setting out on life anew.

Patient sew'r! what wrongs oppress thee!
Glutted to excess, we dine;
With tasks Herculean perplex thee,
At unseemly times we vex thee,
And frustrate thy high design.

But around the deep mucosa
Other structures closely cling,
Nerve and muscle fibres blending,
Fine elastic tissue lending
Strength and firmness to the ring.

Each performs a special function,
Each has secrets of its own.
Have they rivalries to smother?
Do they whisper one another
What is known to them alone?

Primæ viæ, ductus vitæ,
Let them scorn thy use who can;
Source of radiant health and beauty,
I my homage pay, and duty—
Thou it is that makes the man!

—*Canada Lancet.*

## L'OFFRANDE DU CŒUR, OR THE LADY ANATOMIST.

So fair is her face, and so classic her brow,
    No pen can her beauty portray;
But in vain do the graces her figure endow,
She is cold as a vestal, though bound by no vows
    And she casts adulation away.

From her lips scientific the words that are heard
    Seem to issue direct from her brains;
Like Minerva, whose owl she has always preferred,
Regarding it as a superior bird
    To the doves Cytherea maintains.

Yet low at her feet see the youngster that sighs,
    And offers her jewels and gold ;
While in piteous strains with entreaties he plies
To gain. — were it only a glance from her eyes,
    Yet he obdurate finds her, and cold.

But let me interpret thy silence aright ; —
    "I knew I was wrong from the start, —
Thine esteem for this gold and these jewels is light,—
Mere wealth can afford thy pure soul no delight : —
    Then I offer thee, dearest, my heart."

A gratified flash from her eyes he observes.
  And he can but rejoice at the sight.
" 'Tis just what I wanted — blood-vessels and nerves,
And muscles contracting in regular curves !
  I'm obliged to you, really, sir, quite !

"Then I offer thee, dearest my heart."

" I'll examine your auricles, ventricles, too
  (While the muscles relax and contract),
And the valves that the swift-flowing blood passes through.
And I'll see what the chordæ tendineæ do,
  And how the papillæ must act.

And since you're so free with your heart, I suppose
   That your lungs you will also donate,
With the air-cells and bronchial tubes they enclose ;
I'll keep them in spirits" — But here he arose
   With his love metamorphosed to hate.

"I'll be blowed if you will!"

"I'll be blowed if you will !"—it was all he could say,
   Though his feelings tumultuous raged.
So he bowed a farewell ; but he called the same day
On another young lady just over the way,
Who didn't anatomy study, and they,
   In less than a week, were engaged.

—Lonard's Medical Journal.

# HEART DISEASE.

###### BY JAMES B. BURNET, M. D.

"I list, as thy heart and ascending aorta
Their volumes of valvular harmony pour,
And my soul, from that muscular music has caught a
New life, 'mid its dry anatomical lore.

"Oh ! rare is the sound, when thy ventricles throb
In a systolic symphony, measured and slow,
While the auricles answer with rythmical sob
As they murmur a melody wondrously low.

"Oh ! thy cornea, love, has the radiant light
Of the sparkle that laughs in the icicle's sheen,
And thy crystalline lens, like a diamond bright,
Through the quivering frame of thine iris is seen.

" And thy retina, spreading its lustre of pearl,
Like a far-away nebula, distantly gleams
From a vault of black cellular mirrors, that hurl
From their hexagon angles the silvery beams.

"Oh ! the flash of those orbs is enslaving me still,
As they roll 'neath thy palpebræ, dimly translucent,
Obeying, in silence, the magical will
Of the oculo-motor—pathetic—abducent.

"Oh ! sweet is thy voice, as it sighingly swells
From thy daintily quivering chordæ vocales,
Or rings in clear tones from the echoing cells
Of the antrum, the ethmoid, and sinus frontales.

And stately the heave of thy maidenly breast
As the swell of the billow soft rolling to land,
And as soft the vesicular sigh in thy chest
As the sound of the ripple that ebbs o'er the sand.

"But alas! 'tis with many forebodings I pen
Anatomical verses thy beauty to praise,

"Thou hast stepped between me and my skeleton grim,
  Oh lady! fair lady! why crossed you my path?"

For I fear that my studies will never again
Bring the solace they gave in happier days.

"Thou hast stolen the charm from my studio dim,
From dissection I turn with embittering wrath;
Thou hast stepped between me and my skeleton grim,
Oh lady! fair lady! why crossed you my path?"

## VOCAL DYNAMICS.

The human lungs reverberate sometimes with great velocity,
When windy individuals indulge in much verbosity;
They have to twirl the glottis sixty thousand times a minute,
And push and pinch the diaphragm as though the deuce was in it.

CHORUS.

The pharynx now goes up;
The larynx, with a slam,
Ejects a note
From out the throat,
Pushed by the diaphragm.

## THE ARTICULATIONS.

The following arrangement of the names descriptive of the various articulations is by Dr. James L. Little, Professor of Surgery in the University of Vermont.

Enarthrosis, bone to bone,
Femur, acetabulum;
Ginglymus, the hinge I see,
Forwards, backwards swings the knee.
Arthrodia, near the end,
Glide along the foot and hand;
Synchondrosis, we allege,
Calls for costal cartilage;
Syndesmosis — ligament,
Binding bone to bone is meant.
Syssarcosis — lower jaw,
Flesh from ribs to scapula.

Suture, a stitch withal,
Coronal, lambdoid, sagittal.
Harmonia—Tipperary
Rhymes with supramaxillary.
Schindylesis — plowing done --
Vomer in the sphenoid bone.
Gomphosis sets all things right,
Tooth in socket pretty tight.

---

## RISORIUS SANTORINI.

The risorius of Santorini consists of a narrow bundle of fibres,
which arises in the fascia over the masseter muscle, and passing
horizontally forwards, is inserted into the angles of the mouth
joining with the fibres of the depressor anguli oris.  It is placed
superficial to the platysma, and is broadest at its outer extremity.  This muscle varies much in size and form.

*—Gray's Anatomy.*

Risorius Santorini, thee I sing;
Close to the corners of the mouth you cling;
And honest laughter with its cheery ring,
And scornful sneers, with angry, caustic sting,
By thy quick action into being spring.
All kinds of laughter into life you bring,
Light as the dew upon the hum-bird's wing,
Strong as the threefold cord, quick as a flash,
Soft as the breath of music, loud as orchestral crash,
Tender as love, harsh as the breath of hate,
Sad with despair, with brightest hope elate,
Melting with pity, cruel with fiendish scorn,
Darker than midnight, lovelier than the morn,

Wreathing an angel's prayer, blighted with sin,
Whispering peace, mocking with angry din,
Curved in a blessing, curled in hateful curse,
Making good better, making evil worse,

" Risorius Santorini, stand up and laugh ! "

Golden with wisdom, lighter than empty chaff,
Risorius Santorini, stand up and laugh !

—*Medical Bulletin.*

# FOR YE STUDENT MEN.

## THE STUDENT'S ALPHABET.

Oh, A was an artery, filled with injection;
And B was a brick, never caught at dissection.
C were some chemicals, lithium and borax;
D played the deuce with the bones of the thorax.

CHORUS.—

*Taken in short-hand with minute accuracy.*
Fol de rol lol,
Fol de rol lay,
Fol de rol, tol de rol, tol de rol, lay.

E was an embryo in a glass case;
And F a foramen that pierced the skull's base.
G was a grinder, who sharpen'd the tools ;
And H means the half-and-half drunk at the schools.
Fol de rol, etc.

I was some iodine, made of sea-weed;
J was a jolly cock, not used to read.
K was some kreosote, much over-rated;
And L was the lies which about it were stated.
Fol de rol lol, etc.

M was a muscle, cold, flabby and red;
And N was a nerve, like a bit of white thread.
O was some opium, a fool chose to take;
And P were the pins used to keep him awake.
Fol de rol lol, etc.

Q was the quacks, who cure stammer and squint.
R was raw from a burn, and wrapped close in lint.
S was a scalpel, to cat bread and cheese;
And T was a tourniquet, vessels to squeeze.
    Fol de rol lol, etc.

U was the unciform bone of the wrist.
V was the vein which a blunt lancet missed.
W was wax from a syringe that flowed;
X, the 'xaminers, who may be blowed !
    Fol de rol lol, etc.

Y stands for you all, with best wishes sincere;
And Z for the zanies who never touch beer.
So we've got to the end, not forgetting a letter;
And those who don't like it may grind up a better.
              —*London Medical Student.*

---

## A WARNINGE TO YE STUDENT MEN.

*A Ballad of the Sixteenth Century.*

BY DR. WM. TOD HELMUTH, NEW YORK CITY.

Up towne there dwelt a student man,
Tall, straighte and lithe of limbe,
And a prettie serving maide she dwelt
Right opposite to him.

One evening faire ye student man
Was studying aye so hard,
He saw ye prettie serving maide
A-walkinge in ye yard.

Ye student man, he coughed and spat,
And coughed and spat againe,
Till one would thinke his chest was sore
With dreadfule, horrid paine.

Yet still ye prettie serving maide
Walked up a-down ye yarde,
And as she wente she heard ye man
A-coughing aye so harde.

At lengthe she raised her shining eyes
(Bright orbs and mightie cleare),
And shot them at ye student man
Till he felte wondrous queere.

It was ye houre of evening gray,
And dusk fell on ye towne;
One railroade car had erst gone up,
Ye other had gone downe.*

Ye prettie serving maide one eve,
When mirthful to the brim,
Up raised her taper finger-tip
And beckoned unto him.

Ye student man was tall and straighte,
And beautiful was he,
"Awhat it is she wants of me,
Straightway I mean to see."

He crossed ye railroade in ye street,
And entered in ye yarde,
Ye prettie serving maid—she said
"Why cough you aye so harde?"

---

*Street railroads in the Sixteenth Century is an anachronism readily
excused by poetic license.

Ye student man straighte took her hande,
He looked straighte in her eye—
"Because I love you aye so much
Fain would I for ye die."

With that ye student man he hugged
Her bodie all around,
And kissed her redde and pouting lips
With heartie smacking sounde.

"My prettie serving maide," said he,
"Now will I make thee mine,
And you shall feed on strawberries,
And milke and cake and wine."

"Now, student man," ye maiden said,
"Wilt make me great and rich?
Fain I must tell, for seven long years
I've gotten bad the itch."

Up rose ye gallant student man
"Now where, oh! tell me true?"
She held her fingers to ye light
And scratched them black and blue.

Ye student man was all awroth,
A mightie oath swore he;
And all ye while ye serving maide
Did laugh with merrie glee.

"Oh, naughty serving maide," he said,
"O! never worse was founde."
She placed her thumbe upon her nose
And twirled her fingers rounde.

Full four weeks time have passed, and yet
Ye student man he laye,
With sulphur ointment on his limbs,
A-scratching night and day.

And all night long ye student man
Sent up one plaintive cry—
This was ye burthen of ye song,
"Oh! give me sulphur high."

Ye doctor came and rubbed him up,
Ye nurse he rubbed him downe,
Ye serving maide she came and twirled
Her fingers rounde and rounde.

And when ye student man arose,
All worn to bone and skin,
Ye student men they laugh to think
How Sallie took him in.

But ever and anon at night,
When sleeping on ye bed,
Ye night-mare of ye serving maide
Comes flitting through his head.

And then ye student man begins
A scratching, aye so harde,
And thinks he views ye serving maide
A walking in ye yarde.

So student men take heed of this,
Ye lesson of ye songe;
And if she walketh in ye yard,
Why—*let her walke alonge.*

## CHARGE OF THE "PLUCKED" BRIGADE.*

BY A SURVIVOR.

*Dedicated to his Fallen Comrades.*

Right along. right along,
Right along onward,
All in that fearful room
Went half a hundred.
"Forward the 'Plucked' Brigade !
Charge for the 'bus'!" R*nd said,
Into that fearful room
    Went the half hundred.

"Forward the 'Plucked' Brigade !"
Every man was there dismayed,
For each one knew
He had fearfully blundered.

* This parody, though easily understood by many physicians, would not be clear, in all its subtleties, without the following brief explanation : In some of the eastern medical colleges it is customary to allow candidates for graduation, who have failed to pass the regular examination, to come up a second time. This second examination is made in the presence of the entire faculty, and is called the "omnibus," using the word in its original meaning ; the *students*, however, always use the word in its ordinary sense and abbreviate it usually to "bus." A student who passes in this second examination is said to "go through in the 'bus." A few definitions will suffice to make clear remaining points—"Plucked" means "pulled," *i. e.* rejected : "Dutch" courage is, of course, whisky : "*Nunc est bibendum.*"—(Horace) "now let's get drunk ;" "$2 50," the amount refunded to rejected candidates, made up of graduation fee ($30), and the student's contribution to the Commencement expenses ($2 50).

Theirs not to make reply—
For they knew the reason why—
Theirs but to push and try:
Into the omnibus
    Surged the half hundred.


P*nc**st to right of them,
W*ll*ce to left of them,
"Old Gr*ss in front of them,
By turns quizzed and thundered,
Fired at with lymph and pus,
Fetus, os, and musculus,
Into the omnibus
    Charged half a hundred.


Flashed their eyes with courage ("Dutch,")
Flashed, as just beyond their touch
They see the spoils they hope to clutch;
Charging a faculty, while
All the world wondered.
Plunged in the midst of doubt,
Right or wrong they must get out;
R*nd, M**gs, and B*ddl*
Reeled and were put to rout
Non-plussed, out-numbered!
Then they slid out; but not,
    Not the half hundred.


P*nc**st to left of them,
W*ll*ce to right of them,
"Old Gr*ss" behind them,
Grumbled and thundered.

Sent forth without degree--
Not one might style himself M. D.--
They who should no diploma see
Came from that fearful room,
Came from that place of doom,
All that was left of them—
　　Of the half hundred.

When can their glory fade!
O the wild replies they made,
The whole college wondered!
Honor the "Plucked" Brigade,
Honor the charge they made,
Noble half hundred.
　　　　　"Nunc est bibendum:"　$32.50.

# THE DOCTOR HIMSELF.

## TO A PHYSICIAN.

O ! watched for, longed for, through the heavy hours
Of pain and weakness, what a gift is thine !
What a proud science, Godlike and benign !
To pour on withering life sweet mercy's showers,
And on the drooping mind's exhausted powers
Like a revivifying sunbeam shine ;
For thy next smile what sleepless eyelids pine !
What sinking hearts to which the summer flowers
Can breathe no joy ! How many a day
I heard thy footsteps come and die away,
And clung unto that sound as if the earth,
With all its tones of melody and mirth,
To me had naught of interest—nothing worth
The brief, bright moments of thy kindly stay.

—*Medical Herald.*

## THE PHYSICIAN.

### BY H. ERICHSEN, M. D.

Hail to the doctor !  On he toils
    In happy and in weary days;
His enemy, Grim Death, he foils
    And full of hardships are his ways.

They lead from scenes of agony
　To scenes of joy and happiness,
From death-bed which is irony
　Upon the doctor's helplessness,


To cradles filled with human buds
　Which will become the flowers fair,
That fill the world with happiness;
　Or scatter poison everywhere.
Within his bosom hidden lie
　The secrets by his patients told,
And vainly would a person try
　To make him tell by force or gold.


He soothes the pain and heals the wounds
　Made by disease or furious foe,
Or by Time's swift pursuing hounds,
　Who bite the men unless they go
Their way toward the distant end
　O'er stony path with restless zeal;
Nor can a friend assistance lend
　To keep the hounds from off their heel.


You smile and don't believe the tale
　Of that wild, everlasting race.
Look at the old, for every bite
　There is a furrow in the face.
The book of history is o'er-filled
　With names of heroes crowned with fame
Because in battle they have killed
　Their fellow-beings; such win fame.

Not so the doctor, he saves life;
    And in the fever stricken land
He shows what heroism is,
    And through disease with steady hand
He leads his patient.  "All is safe"
    He finally whispers, glad the more
That he has saved another life.
    God bless the doctor o'er and o'er !

---

## THE DOCTOR'S DREAM.

I am sitting alone, by the surgery fire, with my pipe alight,
    now the day is done;
The village is quiet, the wife's asleep, the child is hushed, and
    the clock strikes one!
And I think to myself, as I read the Journal, and I bless my
    life for the peace upstairs,
That the burden's sore for the best of men, but few can dream
    what a doctor bears;
For here I sit at the close of a day, whilst others have counted
    their profit and gain,
And I have tried as much as a man can do, in my humble man-
    ner, to soften pain;
I've warned them all, in a learned way, of careful diet, and
    talked of tone,
And when I have preached of regular meals, I've scarcely had
    time to swallow my own.
I was waked last night in my first long sleep, when I crawled
    to bed from my rounds—dead beat,
"Ah, the Doctor's called!" and they turned and snored, as my
    trap went rattling down the street!

I sowed my oats, pretty wild they were, in the regular manner
    when life was free;
For a medical student isn't a saint, any more than your ortho-
    dox Pharisee!

"I am sitting alone, by the surgery fire, with my pipe alight."

I suppose I did what others have done, since the whirligig round
    of folly began;
And the ignorant pleasures I loved as a boy, I have pretty well
    cursed since I came to be man.

But still I recall through the mist of years. and through the portals of memory steal.

The kindly voice of a dear old man who talked to us lads of the
men who heal.

Of the splendid mission in life for those who study the science
that comes from God.

Who buckle the armor of Nature on. who bare their breasts and
who kiss the rod.

So the boy disappeared in the faith of the man, and the oats
were sowed, but I never forgot

There were few better things in the world to do than to lose all
self in the doctor's lot.

So I left life that had seemed so dear, to earn a crust that isn't
so cheap,

And I bought a share of a practice here, to win my way, and to
lose my sleep;

To be day and night at the beck and call of men who ail and women who lie;

To know how often the rascals live, and see with sorrow the
dear ones die;

To be laughed to scorn as a man who fails, when nature pays
her terrible debt;

To give a mother her first-born's smile. and leave the eyes of the
husband wet;

To face and brave the gossip and stuff that travels about through
a country town;

To be thrown in the way of hysterical girls, and live all terrible
scandals down;

To study at night in the papers here of new disease and of
human ills;

To work like a slave for a weary year. and then to be cursed
when I send my bills!

* * *

Upon my honor, we're not too hard on those who cannot afford
to pay.

For nothing I've cured the widow and child, for nothing I've
watched till the night turned day;

I've earned the prayers of the poor, thank God, and I've borne
the sneers of the pampered beast,

I've heard confessions and kept them safe as a sacred trust like
a righteous priest.

To do my duty I never have sworn, as others must do in this
world of woe,

But I've driven away to the bed of pain, through days of rain,
through nights of snow.

\* \* \*

As here I sit and I smoke my pipe, when the day is done and the
wife's asleep,

I think of that brother-in-arms who's gone, and utter—well
something loud and deep!

And I read the Journal and I fling it down, and I fancy I hear
in the night that scream

Of a woman who's crying for vengeance! Hark! no, the house is
still! It's a doctor's dream!

*—Punch.*

## QUACKS AND DOCTORS.

### BY R. GLISAN, M. D., PORTLAND, OREGON.

I shall, my friends, your kind indulgence ask
Whilst I in humble rhyme attempt the task
On subjects grave a little while to sing,
And hope 'twill not on me your censure bring.

"The doctors have combined," I hear men say,
"In bodies strong, to make their patients pay
Yet higher fees for services and skill
When people poor as we are sadly ill."

Thank God, we can for our society claim
No ignominious, but a noble aim.
Unlike the "union strikes" throughout our land,
The general good we seek, and not to band
Ourselves to force submission to commands
Of selfish gain; nor yet to make demands
Upon the people, or the public purse,
That we some pet or tainted scheme may nurse,
As corporations vast too often do,
As well as other combinations too.

Protective tariffs? No! nor patent rights
We seek; protection only from those blights,
The quacks, who, locust-like, infest the land
By thousands. They upon street corners stand,
With smooth and oily tongues, or blatant cries,
Retail their salves, their poisons, and their lies.

These daring tricksters do no means forego
With cunning skill to thrive on human woe!
They sing, they shout, or plead in silver tone
Till gaping few in number great have grown,
To see the flippant tongue of art and wile
Like fatal snare their victims soon beguile.

At first, like shoals of fish, the crowd do wait,
Then rush in haste to try deceptive bait;
Though sometimes — as aquatic birds on wing —
In circles small or vast, in flight do swing,

Suspecting all they see, and flying shy
Of danger, till some bright decoy they spy,
Then they the doubtful spot no longer shun,
And soon are victims of the sportsman's gun;
Thus silly crowds, like birds by wooden duck,
Misled by buyers false, the quack doth pluck.

But quacks there are of many sorts and kinds,
As dupes we see of many grades and minds.
One class ignore the rostrum, but presume
To claim all honors.  Titles they assume
More noble far than those conferred by prince
Or king, in palmy days of yore, or since.
They fill with false certificates of cure
The press; and oft from men of sense secure
Endorsement.  How and why, I must confess,
Are problems solved by nothing I can guess.

Thus fortified, from place to place they rush,
False hopes inspire, which time, alas! must crush;
Then, like the "Kansas hoppers," disappear,
When all things green are nipped, both far and near.

If laws protective shall not e'er be found
To cunning wiles and tricks of quacks confound,
Then plain our duty.  Shall we hesitate
The public mind at large to educate
Upon deceptions which concern us all,
When sick, the young and old, both great and small?
If such a course alone to us remains,
Humanity at stake, let's spare no pains.

Yet some there are, although not quacks by name,
For purpose useful still they are the same,

Who play the dodge of always something new
In drugs or skill, and only known by few,
To please the fancy of the present age,
When novelty, not worth, is all the rage—
The good, if new, they say we must abide.

And some, to gain applause, that men may stare
And say, " Behold, the doctor over there
A genius is," ignore all business sense,
Which, after all, is only common sense;
Be doctor void of this, no art or trick
By him inspires my confidence when sick.

And others, who both guile and trick disown,
Yet always changing, and forever prone
To rush from this to that, and try, by turn,
All remedies; and all, in time, to spurn.

As maid, by fickle dame of fashion led,
Sleek ringlets tries, and then a frizzled head;
A bonnet first she dons, and next a hat,
Too small for baby doll or pussy cat.

One day in crinoline, in shape a cone,
In circle, vast as belt of torrid zone;
Next day in skirt as long as railroad train,
That westward bound, or eastward, sweeps the plain.
At times in modest costume, like the quail,
And then in peacock's plumage she doth sail.

Self-doubting souls we find, who ne'er depend
On judgment save of others, who commend
In language bold whatever they extol,
From drugs of magic power—to charcoal.

These modest souls are like an open boat
Adrift on river, or at sea afloat,
Devoid of rudder, steersman, captain—all,
When low'ring clouds portend a dreadful squall.
For rudder, self-reliance they but need;
For captain, judgment sound, to take the lead.

'Tis strange that men and women oft intrust
The sacred things of home to him, whom trust
They would not even for a monthly rent
Of room, or house, or loan of dime or cent.

The man who drives their coach or livery team,
And he who regulates the boiler's steam
Of ship, or boat, or fleeter railroad car,
Or pilot on Columbia's dreaded bar.
Or mender of a watch, or clock, or ring,
Or hat, or boots—in short, of anything.
Must duly sober seem, or be displaced
Before his task is done, and feel disgraced;
Yet he who claims the power to regulate
Machines divine, the most elaborate
Of God's sublimest works, may tippling be,
And hardly know the land from rippling sea,
And still be sought to cure his fellow-men;
This puzzle solve if any of you can.

In honor pure and spotless as the gems
Of rarest kind that shine in diadems
Of famous ruler, whether king or queen,
Or, as the snow on mountain heights is seen,
Should be the man whose art and calling tend
To give him knowledge all of things that lend
To homely life an ever sacred charm,
Or fill the soul with sadness and alarm.

He should in morals be a paragon
E'en though he hail from " web-foot Oregon."
And he must sacred in his bosom hide
The things that patient may in him confide.

His knowledge deep as ocean's mighty bed,
And broad as universal space o'erhead
Must be; else like a shallow, narrow stream
It drieth up when hot the sun doth beam.

No hobbies should he ever wish to ride,
Nor should he float at random with the tide
Of public favor, truth should be his aim,
E'en though he miss the goal of worldly fame.

A student must he always try to be,
And think not merely of his paltry fee,
In all improvements being wide awake,
And gilded brass for gold should ne'er mistake.

The doctor true and wise doth sift and weigh
All things himself, well knowing what he may
From others use as truths, and what discard
As worthless trash, deserving no regard.

When deeply ploughed the scientific field
Doth many grains of wheat quite often yield,
Though when the surface one but slightly chafes,
The soil more chaff than golden grain vouchsafes.

If ink were blood, from human victims ta'en,
No place too vast to hold the thousands slain
To furnish it, and loud would be the groans
Of bleeding, dying men for worthless tomes.

Yet vast our knowledge and improvements now
In science and the arts, we must allow,
To what they were a hundred years ago:
Yet vaster still, a hundred more, we know.

To us the ken advancing science may
Then grant to glance along the sun's bright ray,
And objects small and large, both far and near,
Discern; which now, unseen, may our career
As sudden stop as clock by earthquake shock,
Or vessel swift, when hurled against a rock,
Or human life, by apoplectic stroke,
Or lightning's message, when the wire is broke,

No true advance can physic ever make,
If theories for facts we mostly take;
Our knowledge must with practice always join,
For gold without alloy would make soft coin.

Whilst we our science seek to elevate,
Fraternal feelings we should cultivate;
Opposing and discordant motions mar,
Obstruct, impede, the scientific car,
Which slowly moves in sparsely-settled lands,
E'en when untrammeled by impeding bands.

Though ever slow the car of science be,
Its progress must be sure if all agree,
To work in harmony.   However poor
The scanty means on our Pacific shore,
Some things there are that we may do,
Far better here than those in lands less new,

To speed the car on new centennial track.
So when, in future years, our sons look back
Upon our actions, they will shed no tears
At slothful deeds of father pioneers.

The laws of miasms and contagions may
By country doctors best be known: away
From crowded haunts of city or large town,
This open field is ours to seek renown.
Not sluggards let us be; the great Northwest
Demands that we, her sons, shall do our best.

As clouds are pierced by Hood and Ranier peaks.
So youthful vigor to ourselves bespeaks
A grandly glorious and exalted stand,
As scientists attain in any land.

Our minds shall, like our crystal mountain streams,
Be sparkling clear, reflecting golden beams
As dazzling bright, if faithful we but run,
As those of diamond, star, or noonday sun.

Let fools and boobies our profession jeer,
Or jealous scientists our calling sneer:
Let editors and lawyers, in mere fun,
Fire off their little squibs and ready pun;
In lieu of better words nickname us "pills,"
Or, more degrading still, but call us "squills."

Let debtors to our goodness, in pure spite,
A free and lengthy service to requite.
Our skill in question call behind our backs,
Us for malpractice sue, and dub us quacks.

When we perchance essay poetic rhyme,
But lack the needful aid, the spark divine,
And seek the shady grove where muses dwell,
Let them with haughty airs our hopes dispel,
And say: "The man who deals with human ills,
Can only sigh, and think of human chills."

When inspiration's fire his soul might rack,
His cry would be, "Pray give me ipecac."
Apollo's friend, Laconian Hyacinth,
Suggests to him the name of colocynth.
A rhyme might call for heavenly manna,
Which he would chime with salts and senna.

The morning sun the twinkling stars doth pale
Would rhyme to him with, "Take a little ale;"
Come, soar aloft, and tread the milky way,
With, "Oh, my friend, do try some wine and whey;"
Those realms above where angels love to walk,
With, "Acid stomach needs both milk and chalk."

Let poets wander far in space above,
And only dream of beauty, stars and love;
Or sing the praise of Jupiter and Mars,
Or chant heroic deeds of bloody wars;
Or tune their harps into a soft refrain,
To charm the heart of loving maid or swain;
Or think in verse of Adam's Paradise,
Before the infant world was stained by vice;
Of Noah's safety ark, which rode the flood,
And from a drowning world preserved the good;
Of Grecian art and deeds of mighty Rome,
Which charmed and thrilled the world from zone to zone:

Or sing in martial tunes of famous Gaul
Whose arms in war bade fair the world t' inthrall;
Or soar along beyond the bounds of time,
Behold the end, the last great crash sublime;
The day when planets from their orbits fly
And dart like rockets through the lurid sky,
When orbs of Heaven, and the fires of hell,
Through space unlimited, shall rush pell-mell.

Let muses all and all the sons of men
From every land and clime chime in, "Amen:"
The modest doctor still our homes will guard,
Although ignored he be by muse and bard.

When pain, despair, and secret shafts of death
In troops combined, as thieves by night, in stealth,
Life's portals enter—hurl their poisoned darts,
Then helpless lie the jewels of our hearts
Until the doctor comes, applies a balm,
And bids our stricken souls be calm.

Shall laureled heroes of a million slain
In war more honors from the world obtain
Than surgeons brave and skilled, who thousands save
From pangs in life, and an untimely grave?

'Tis passing strange that honors always crown
The lucky hero, whether king or clown.
The man of science may the world unfold,
And author be of blessings rare, untold;
The hero's fame will ring from shore to shore
And drown the higher claims of him of lore.

If there no heroes be but sons of Mars,
Then brighter diamonds are than heavenly stars.

Is honor rather found in warlike strife
Than in the God-like acts of saving life?

The cannon's deafening roar that shakes the plain
The awe-struck mind of man doth so enchain.
That honor is not seen in common deeds,
The dazzled soul the stunning noise but heeds.

The God of physic was by lightning slain.
That fabled Pluto might more souls obtain;
His pupils now the power to raise the dead
Claim not, but only life prolong instead.

As agents human of this world below.
By God allowed to lessen pain and woe.
They fight the silent. miasmatic breath.
That poisons blood and brain, and leads to death.

In acts like these are seen, all else apart.
Heroic deeds that stir and move the heart;
For subtle dangers courage true and rare
Require. divested of all gloss, all glare.

The doctor must with valor be endowed
To meet the evils which his path do crowd;
Be ever ready duty to perform
By day, by night, through snow, through flood and
        storm;
His art and skill to every class and sect
Must be extended; none he should neglect.

The poor and rich alike require his aid.
In lowly huts, or mansions broad o'erlaid
In marble—whether low or high their station.
From every land, from every clime and nation.

The infant frail in home's fraternal arms,
The soldier brave, whom cannon ball disarms,
The nerve-sick woman, and the heart-sick maid
Whom dart of Cupid *hors du combat* laid,

The man of God, with soul serene and calm,
The hardened sinner, careless of the balm
Which faith in Christ to wounded hearts doth bring,
That faith from which the deeds of goodness spring,
The storm-tossed seaman on the mighty main,
Or wounded landsman on the bloody plain,
Require alike the doctor's ready aid
When sickness doth their vital parts pervade.

All scenes and dangers he must bravely face,
The hidden poisons that our frames embrace
From lowlands of a miasmatic shore,
And lightning's vivid glare, or battle's roar.

His knowledge, too, of ready kind must be;
For books, as guides to read, no time has he
When called to accidents of limb or life;
Else, snapped in twain by the unequal strife,
The slender chord that binds our flesh and souls
Must surely, quickly be, by fiendish ghouls —
Death's angels—who around, with silent wing,
The sick do fly, on fleeting souls to spring.

The doctor may assume a gentle mien
At death-bed scenes, be quiet and serene;
Though full of sympathy, yet self-possessed,
No trepidation he should manifest;
Still, times there are when human heart and soul
Give way to grief in spite of self-control.

Than mortal less or more must be the man
Who claims the power to heal, who griefless can
Behold his patient sinking low in pain.
When he his skill and art has tried in vain;
Or see a brother, father, mother, all,
Of helpless girl, by pestilence to fall,
When he with boasted science vainly tries
To stay the hand of death that he espies;
Or see a husband young, himself beside,
At sudden loss of her, his lovely bride,
When flick'ring flame of life, alas is fled,
Despairing ask, "O, doctor, is she dead?"

Sad proof these scenes that mortals frail we are,
Still, God our aid, we many lives may spare.
Let us by help of Him our efforts bend
To fight the common foe to bitter end,
And faithful to our duties let us stand
When pestilence and famine stalk the land;
To poor and rich alike our help to lend,
Till death from life our own frail souls shall rend.

—*Oregon Medical Journal.*

## BISHOPS AND DOCTORS.

I am not ashamed to say I have a son a doctor.— *Speech of the Bishop of Liverpool to medical men.*

How kind of the Bishop, and how patronizing,
And yet to his Punch 'tis a little surprising,
That, speaking to medical men there in session,
He dared speak of shame and a noble profession.

A bishop looks after our souls, but how odd is
The sneer that's implied at the curers of bodies;
For surely it would be no hard task to fish up
A hundred brave doctors as good as the Bishop.

—Punch.

---

## THE GOOD PHYSICIAN.

BY DR. OLIVER WENDELL HOLMES.

How blest is he who knows no meaner strife
Than art's long battle with the foes of life!
No doubt assails him, doing still his best,
And trusting kindly Nature for the rest;
No mocking conscience tears the thin disguise
That wraps his breast, and tells him that he lies.
He comes:  the languid sufferer lifts his head
And smiles a welcome from his weary bed;
He speaks: what music like the tones that tell
"Past is the hour of danger—all is well!"
How can he feel the petty stings of grief
Whose cheering presence always brings relief?
What ugly dreams can trouble his repose
Who yields himself to soothe another's woes?
Hour after hour the busy day has found
The good physician on his lonely round;
Mansion and hovel, low and lofty door
He knows, his journeys every path explore—
Where the cold blast has struck with deadly chill
The sturdy dweller on the storm-swept hill;

Where by the stagnant marsh the sickening gale
Has blanched the poisoned tenants of the vale,
Where crushed and maimed the bleeding victim lies,
Where madness raves, where melancholy sighs,
And where the solemn whisper tells too plain
That all his science, all his art were vain.

How sweet his fireside when the day is done,
And cares have vanished with the setting sun!
Evening at last its hour of respite brings,
And on his couch his weary length he flings.

Soft be thy pillow, servant of mankind,
Lulled by an opiate art could never find;
Sweet be thy slumber—thou hast earned it well—
Pleasant thy dreams! Clang! Goes the midnight bell!
Darkness and storm! The home is far away
That waits his coming ere the break of day;
The snow clad pines their wintry plumage toss—
Doubtful the frozen stream his road must cross;
Deep lie the drifts, the slanted heaps have shut
The hardy woodman in his mountain hut—
Why should thy softer frame the tempest brave?
Hast thou no life, no health, to lose or save?

Look! Read the answer in his patient's eyes—
For him no other voice when suffering cries;
Deaf to the gale that all around him blows,
A feeble whisper calls him—and he goes.

Or seek the crowded city—Summer's heat
Glares burning, blinding in the narrow street;
Still, noisome, deadly, sleeps the envenomed air;
Unstirred the yellow flag that says "beware!"
Tempt not thy fate—one little moment's breath
Bears on its viewless wings the seeds of death.

Thou at whose door the gilded chariots stand,
Whose dear-bought skill unclasps the miser's hand,
Turn from thy fatal quest, nor cast away
That life so precious; let a meaner prey
Feed the destroyer's hunger; live to bless
Those happier homes that need thy care no less!
Smiling he listens; has he then a charm
Whose magic virtues peril can disarm?
No safeguard this, no amulet he wears.
Too well he knows that Nature never spares
Her truest servant, powerless to defend
From her own weapons her unshrinking friend.
He dares the fate the gravest well might shun,
Nor asks reward save only Heaven's "well done!"
Such are the toils, the perils that he knows,
Days without rest and nights without repose,
Yet all unheeded for the love he bears
His art, his kind, whose every grief he shares.

*—Centennial Anniversary Poem.*


## THE DOCTOR.

BY E. J. BLAIR, CAMBRIDGE, OHIO.

"A wit's a feather, and a chiefs a rod;
An honest man's the noblest work of God."

So wrote the poet Pope; whose genius still
Shines forth from the distant past and ever will.
We quote his work on man, perhaps the best
He ever wrote; superior to the rest

In many points:  We, following his plan,
Would make our theme some species of the man,
And, though no poet, treat it as we can.

'Twould be presumption in a man like me,
Raised in the backwoods 'neath a forest-tree,
A peasant of the peasants, rural born.
Whose struggles started with his natal morn,
To dare attempt the highest realms of thought
And stir you up by fancies, quaintly wrought.
Oh, no! an easier, plainer task be mine;
I'll take the doctor up and let him shine.
His light, devoid of effort on my part,
Will doubtless shine, and no poetic art
Will be required to rivet your attention:
The theme demands it by the very mention.

I hope no personal rancor sways my pen,
Nor malice tugging down at other men;
Now he who has a doctor's manly heart,
Who feels his soul sincere and loves his art,
Who casts all private ends behind his back,
And steadfastly pursues the honest track,
Whose industry irradiates his mind;
Whose soul seeks joy in labors for his kind,
Is more a doctor, far, than he who runs
His pedigree to seven times seven sons,
Or he who holds beneath his costly robe
Diplomas from the four winds of the globe,
They are the great ones—so the farmer's spouse
Raised a great calf—it sucked from several cows.

First, then, I shall describe some poor, mean game,
Obscure, who merit not the doctor's name;

But men will call them doctor, every day,
And hence they do his work and more than take his pay.
Some poor illiterate, senseless as an ox.
But gifted with the cunning of the fox,
Gets a receipt, prepares a pill or plaster,
And then, at once, becomes a mighty master
Of Hygeia's art divine; the Centaur's skill
Withers and fades before his secret pill.

Commencing at the bottom, first we find
The corn and cancer doctor, mole-like, blind,
Who knows one thing alone, some great specific
For warts, moles, cancers, corns and things terrific:
And if you scruple his profound ability,
He jumps about with true toad-like agility.
He shells you out a bucketful of corns,
That he has captured, branches, roots, and horns;
And cancers large as bits of cheese
Which he has taken away,
That puzzled all the doctors round,
For many a long, long day.

Another class of doctors first commence
By plastering notices on the alley fence:
They work on pedagogue Hoofland's Bitters,
They climb the ascending scale of itch and tetters,
Until arriving at the uppermost story
They make the hair-restorative their glory,
And often finish off, 'tis true and queer.
As special doctors of the eye and ear;
And mighty ones they often claim to be
From distant foreign university;
Their anatomic knowledge out of joint,
In other cases they will reach the point.

They know the eye and ear to be two great holes
In which they drop their cure-alls—simple souls.

The plaster brother of the lower order
Dabbles but light, skirts around the border
Of Therapeutia, fearing to invade
Her sombre realms, he keeps within the shade;
As son of parents strict from midnight ball
Returns close crouching to the alley wall,
So he creeps round, he shuns the blaze of day,
And does his business in a private way.

He's a hungry knowledge of the fact
That sales require uncommon zeal and tact;
He knows that he must do some precious lying
To make his living—and there's no use denying
His ready skill and power—so thus he's able
To prove his point—often by well-drawn fable;
His precious plaster is proclaimed with zeal
To draw out pain rheumatic—at the heel,
Will bring the roaring tooth-ache quickly out,
Exterminate a pain, and cure the gout:
After that fact can any person doubt?
It strengthens, too, applied from night till morn,
More than potatoes, cabbage, beef or corn.
No other plaster spreads so soft and slick,
And then it's such a glorious thing to stick,
As often those find out who come to buy it,
Sticks to the pocket and sticks to the part—try it.

The patent-pill men merit some attention,
More worthy than a merely passing mention;
Their name is legion, their pretensions many,
Their methods sly to turn an honest penny;

Their sage announcements cut like two-edged sabres,
The press is daily teeming with their labors;
And, that their labors are not all in vain,
Witness the golden luck of Dr. Jayne,
And Doctor Brandreth, too, his pills, now obsolete,
Retired the doctor to a country seat.


Some smoothly-worded notice takes the eye;
We look it up, we cannot pass it by.
There is something so peculiar in it
That we are almost certain to begin it.
Nothing is plainer than this little fact,
'Tis written well; the author, full of tact,
So slyly leads us on we scarcely see
Where we are going, what it tends to be,
Till, ah ! we reach the summit of the hill,
And stop confounded at the mansion's pill—
The ready pill that always will insure
Two shillings worth of most unfailing cure.
The thing it cures the best,
And keeps from getting worse,
Is that rare and strange disease,
A plethora of the purse.


How modest, too, they are, those men of pills,
In blazing forth their list of human ills;
While we, the readers, blush, alas ! in vain,
To see humanity exposed for gain,
And wonder much that men who know propriety
Would dare such thing and still move in society,
In circles, too, esteemed the very best,
And tolerated—even more—caressed.

In some sly corner, hid from gaze,
"Old Sands of Life" sits down to end his days;
Like the cunning spider, skillfully he weaves
A tale whose fairness multitudes deceives:
At twenty-five his venerable name
Gets in the papers, and it gives him fame,
And, what is more agreeable and funny,
The dupes respond, and poor old Sands gets money.
Then how his venerable soul regales;
How he imbibes good brandies, wines and ales,
How oft the juicy oyster disappears
Down the vast gulf between our hero's ears!
He sports the cane, he wears the stylish hat,
The dupes wax poor, but Sands grows rich and fat.
His finger bears a diamond of first water,
He hopes to marry Shoddy's wealthy daughter,
Who smiles and simpers at his first approach;
He's rich — he drives a thousand dollar coach.

Madame de Humbug, from the torrid zone,
Comes to the States for public good alone;
Sweet peace and virtue fill her lofty mind,
She has no salt for birds, no axe to grind.
Her secret emissaries prowl about
From town to town, on every railroad route,
Hunting their victims, turning every stone,
As bear for crawfish hunts, as dog for bone.
And each to hide herself from human eyes,
Adopts some specious form of neat disguise.
One sells cosmetics, while, perhaps, another
Retails the history of some pious brother,
Who labors in the ministry of pardon,
Wisely and strongly in his master's garden.

She's in the garden, too, we have no doubts,
Her business is to clear away the *sprouts;*
She sells a costly secret more than common,
By which she swindles many a silly woman
Of her loose change; she, meantime, growing wiser
Finds that the good all went to the adviser.

We have all sorts of doctors, ready made,
Like clothing, just to suit the wants of trade;
Each silly fancy that exists on earth
Has given some ology or pathy birth.
Each element is forced to take its part
Twisted and tormented by the chemist's art;
Each temperature from red heat down to snow
Has been employed on mortal man below,
And simple faith in all its naked beauty
Is used to bring the system back to duty.

Hydropathy sets up her claim to cure
All sorts of ailments human frames endure;
Her votaries voluntary naiads make
Of their dear selves for Health's sweet, comely sake,
Nice nymphs Neptunian, though a little spare,
From dining on bran-bread or country air;
At some establishments, 'tis slyly said,
They get a larger share of air than bread:
But, lest I raise some hydropathist's "dander,"
I must confess I think the story slander.
These naiads of the water-cure design
Are often neither to your taste nor mine,
For all the old maids of the Yankee Nation
Seek in those dear retreats regeneration;
And oft they seek the boon with mournful zeal,
Soak, plash, perspire, till toes and fingers peel,

Only to learn the melancholy truth
That health and beauty must depart with youth,
That all the waters of Damascus' streams
Can ne'er restore the object of their dreams:
As, thin of face, and far more light of purse,
They come back home — perhaps a little worse.

The old Thompsonians claim a tribute, too,
Though now, alas! they are a scattered few:
And stark enthusiasts now seldom dream
To practice medicine alone by steam;
Yet once they steamed whole families of sinners,
Raised myriads of diaphragms — spilt countless dinners,
Enlarged on friends by calomel bereft,
And pitched into the doctors right and left.
Lobelia, goddess of the rising meal!
Was their divinity; and to their zeal
Grew great and greater, rising every day,
Until at last it puked itself away.

*—Medical Herald.*

## THE COUNTRY DOCTOR.

*Annual Address before the Connecticut Medical Society, Hartford, Ct., May 24, 1883, by W. G. Brownson, A. M., M. D., New Canaan, Conn.*

Fellows and Brethren of our Commonwealth,
The trusted guardians of the lives and health
Of half a million of our noble race,
Accept the cordial greeting which the place
And the occasion bid us here extend.
Where noble aims and nobler spirits blend.

How fitting to our chosen mission, here
To meet for counsel each recurring year;
To garner up for use the ripened fruit
Of past experience; to wisely suit
The rich and varied lessons of the past
To modern methods, multiform and vast.
How suited to the needs of men of care
To slip the burdens which they daily bear,
To deftly smooth a furrow from the brow,
Refresh each heart, renew each sacred vow,
To stay the whitening of a single hair
On heads too early silvered o'er by care,
To mirror back the smile we here extend,
And cross the palm with many a trusted friend.

By virtue of the office which I bear,
In the behalf of those whose trusts I share,
A hearty welcome let me here extend
To every Fellow, Delegate and Friend.

And now what shall I say,—what can I say
Suited to the occasion and the day?
Among my auditors are hoary men
Already past their three score years and ten,
Who long have honored their respective spheres;
Riper in wisdom than in gathered years.
College professors grace our festal board,
Whose brains and libraries are amply stored;
The learned critics who unravel threads
That sorely puzzle many anxious heads,—
Our happy specialists with scarce a flaw,
Experts in council and in courts of law;
All these, whose rare attainments justly claim
Our grateful recognition of their fame,

Need not our praise; their names and deeds command
Profound respect throughout our native land.

Another class I see, but few are here,
Though adding to our numbers year by year.
Attentive listeners while others teach,
Whose mission is to practice not to preach.
The privates in our noble army band—
The country doctors scattered through the land,
Who bear the knapsack, catch the fiercest fire;
For them I speak—the rest need not retire.

Fresh from the college halls our hero comes
To enter on his work in rural homes.
His recent past seems like a fitful dream;
The weeks of rigid application teem
With memories no future can efface,
No words express, no pencil fitly trace.
The chambers of his memory have been pressed
For lodgement of the knowledge he possessed,
Knowledge of varied kind, diffuse, abstract,
From fine spun theory to settled fact,
Chemical formulas, hygienic laws,
The limits of disease, its hidden cause,
Medical jurisprudence, stale and dry
As skeletons of bare anatomy.
The college quiz and lectures by the score
Embodied in a dozen books or more—
All these, by specious cramming, he must gain
And reproduce, his parchment to obtain.
The ordeal of examination past,
"Accepted" greets his weary eyes at last;

Little he cares that purse is empty now,
A glow of perfect joy rests on his brow.

Rejoice with him who finds a blissful day
To ease the burden of life's devious way,
A ray of light and hope to gild the road
And pierce the veil that shrouds the last abode.
Our young M. D. decides to settle down
For a few years in a small country town,
Hoping, by patient toil, ere long to gain
The richer field to which his hopes attain.

You who have walked the road he enters here
With careful tread, alternate hope and fear,
Each step observed by many eager eyes
That note too soon his frequent fallacies;
You who have known in other days with me
How blessed was the word of sympathy,
Have known and felt when weary and distressed
The need of hope, encouragement and rest,—
Need but the mirror,—not the photograph,
To catch at once the outline of the path.

The months pass on and gather into years;
With each new day some new demand appears;
Demands for knowledge he has not been taught,
Nor read in books, nor gleaned from modern thought.

As in the countless millions of the earth,
From present time back to creation's birth,
No two are found alike in every part,
In form and feature, gifts of mind and heart,
So in our ills the skillful watcher finds
As wide divergence as in forms or minds;

In chronic ones he seeks to know the cause,
And finds it hidden deep in Nature's laws:
Each chapter of life's history must be
Consulted ere he finds the remedy,
Mixed and administered with studied pains,
As brilliant Opie mixed his paints—with brains.

When we consider all the slender strings
From which the melody or discord springs,
When life's frail harp is touched by unseen hands,—
How shall we wisely answer the demands,
Touch the right chord, proffer the needed boon,
And all the harmonies of life attune?

The chains of circumstance with fetters bind
Too oft the best endeavors of the mind.
We seek a remedy for human ill,
Where neither pharmacist's nor doctor's skill
Finds the elixir that can stay the drain
Of wasted energy of nerve and brain.
Unfortunate surroundings it may be,
Or some harsh discord in the family,
Diseased inheritance that poisons life
And fills its days with bitterness and strife,—
Or, worse than all, what hundreds of us see
In many homes—a grinding poverty:
Mothers of babes anæmic, underfed
And over-worked to gain their scanty bread;—
What wonder if we often fail to please
Ourselves, or bring to others strength and ease!
What wonder if we envy our compeers,
Whose city practice through a score of years
Leaves them the care of but the favored few,
With ample means, and readiness to do

The will of the attendant when expressed,
Either for needed change or needed rest!
Some healing waters flow in distant lands.
To test their sovereign virtues, he demands
An extra nurse, a trip across the sea,
A well-filled purse, congenial company,
A cottage by the sea, or mountain air,
Release from labor and relief from care.
How wide the contrasts in our earthly lot,—
How brief the pilgrimage, how soon forgot!

The lessons of experience, as taught
In country practice, oft are dearly bought.
The modest worker in a sterile field,
Needing the scanty harvest it may yield,
Sometimes from doubt, sometimes from anxious fear,
Wishes an able counselor were near.
An only child, within whose tender life
Centre the fondest hopes of husband, wife
And many friends, seems on the verge of death;—
Convulsed with pain, with fitful, rapid breath,
Clenched hands, eyes sunken, nostrils stretching wide—
He scarce can count the pulse's hasty stride.
He looks at his thermometer amazed,
Its column to a frightful figure raised;—
Ah, you and I have felt his anxious fear,
And wished some able counselor were near
To aid in such extremity, or bear
Of such responsibility a share.
No time to lose, he summons to his aid
His nearest rival; time is quickly made,
And, Jehu like, with foaming steed he drives,
And at the moment specified arrives.

In manner brusk, pompous in air and style,
He greets his brother with the blandest smile,
With new found friends shakes hands with relish keen,
Happy to see them, happier to be seen.
His conversation he directs to these,
With studied effort to attract and please:
Tells of an anxious case he had last night,
Which by his skill is coming out all right:
Details his treatment in a learned way.
Bold and heroic, as we sometimes say;
Consults his watch, and softly names the time
When he must see a case with Doctor Prime—
A city lady, wealthy and refined,
Attractive both in person and in mind.
His fine impression made, he condescends
To interview the doctor and the friends;
And, ere he sees the case, states his belief
That he can soon suggest a prompt relief.
He quickly scans the case, and feigns to see
At once the lesion and the remedy;
Tells of a dozen cases he has had
Within a year, with symptoms quite as bad.
And thus the farce of consultation ends;
What further he discloses to the friends
We ne'er shall know; but somehow it transpires,
He gets the case—his brother soon retires.

The quiet meditations of our friend
Upon this strange proceeding and its end
Are like the winds across the dreary plain—
Now harsh and chill, now soft and mild again.
He feels that rank injustice has been done;
He asked for bread, he has received a stone:

He fain would hurl it back, and promptly say,
If called to counsel at some future day,
This wily brother he would sooner see
In everlasting infelicity.
His purse and reputation feel the strain,
His honest heart and character remain.
With firm resolve to do as best he may
The arduous duties of each coming day,
He learns to wait; assured that in the end
He is not poor whose conscience is his friend.

Turn now, and for a moment, let us trace
In happier mood a second anxious case.
Our modest friend, who does not know it all,
Again needs counsel; and within his call,
Retiring for a time for calm repose,
Is one of whose exalted rank he knows.
He thinks an operation must be done;—
He calls upon his friend, the kindly tone
Of cordial welcome which the good man gives,
In part his keen solicitude relieves.
Together to the bedside they repair,
Together scan the case with patient care,
Together then for conference they retire,
As friend with friend, one aim and one desire.
To save the case from an untimely end
The surgeon's knife its services must lend,
And, all arranged, our veteran takes his place
Simply as an assistant in the case.
To wield the knife he modestly declines;
To aid his younger brother he designs;
His very presence nerves the timorous hand
To steady work and ready self command.

With warm congratulations he proceeds;
A hint and a suggestion as he needs,
In undertone so guide, he scarcely knows
That to his blade the riper judgment goes.
Relief obtained, success assured, they share
The honored garlands which the victors wear;
Rejoicing friends their gratitude express
In other ways than simple thankfulness;
Softly aside our learned counsel pays
His younger friend the tribute of his praise,—
Asks him to call and question if need be,
And slips into his hand his handsome fee.

If there be happiness for mortals here,
A sweet symposium where care and fear
May not intrude, our brother now can feel
A heaven, where thieves do not break through nor steal.

And thus alternate light and shadow fall
Across the checkered pathway of us all.
Our lives are like the volumes on our shelves;
Their style and binding show our outer selves;
The gilt or plainer dress our rank or birth;
Still but the printed page can give them worth.

How may we see ourselves, who backward turn
The pages of our life-book, and discern
The country doctor of our boyhood days,
With foes and friends to censure or to praise !
In saddle or in sulky brown and grim,
The storm and darkness were alike to him—
Through weary miles his keen anxiety
And faithful horse his only company;

His saddle-bags and dusty garb might tell
Each aged sire and school-boy knew him well.
As through the window or the open door
They watched his coming at the appointed hour.

When coveted success had eased his brain,
He oft could feel the force of the refrain,
" Three faces wears the doctor: when first sought
An angel's; and a God's, the cure half wrought;
But when, the cure complete, he seeks his fee,
The devil is less terrible than he."
'Twas his to know betimes when he had done
Most faithful service, he had scarce begun
Rejoicing ere the shafts of malice dread,
Like hailstones fell on his defenceless head.

Each day he passed some who from jealousy,
Malice or spite would do him injury;
Each day he stood beside some prostrate form,
Whose outstretched hand and trusting look gave warm
And kindly welcome, while he sought to show
The brighter side and hide the threatened woe.
'Twas his to know the rapture of success;
'Twas his to feel the pangs of bitterness,
When, baffled, he must stand with bated breath,
Dumb and confounded, face to face with death.

We take their places, and survey with pride
The well earned laurels they have laid aside.
If their facilities were less than ours,
We gain advantage, not by added powers
For better service, but by nobler deeds—
More self devotion to our fellows' needs.

Who does his best within his humble field
Has gathered honors which he need not yield
To man or angel; faithful in few things,
He wears the crown which faithful service brings.
None wears another's armor, each his own;
Ours will be measured when our work is done.

The prince of Epics from his classic vale
Beguiles the student with a pleasing tale.
With festive games the populace to please,
In memory of his father Anchises,
Æneas raises with his mighty hand
A lofty mast, round which the people stand;
And on its top, held by a slender string,
There sits a timorous dove with folded wing.
He now invites the archers standing by
To open contest for the mastery:
Four heed the invitation, and prepare
The plaudits and the offered gifts to share.
Then from the well-drawn bow an arrow flies
As lightning cleaves its pathway through the skies;
The quivering mast and flapping wings proclaim
The skilled precision of the archer's aim;
Beneath the captive's feet, still pinioned fast,
The arrowhead lies buried in the mast.
Then ardent Mnestheus next, aiming on high,
Directs alike his arrow and his eye;
His arrow cuts the cord,— the captive flees
Toward the dark clouds, high on the southern breeze.
Quickly Eurytion holds his ready bow,
Calls his lost brother to attest his vow:
Now spied the dove, joyful in azure vault,
His whizzing arrow makes the last assault;

Transfixed, she leaves her life within the sky,
Descending 'mid the shouts of victory,
Down, down to earth, now pinioned fast and warm
The fatal arrow and the lifeless form.
But one remains—the aged archer stands
Viewing the prizes earned by other hands.
All seems accomplished; yet Acestes next
His arrow toward the heavens straightway directs,
It speeds its way athwart the liquid clouds,
When, lo ! a trail of fire its path enshrouds;
On blazing wings it spans the arch on high
Like shooting stars unfastened from the sky;
Till, quite consumed before their wondering eyes,
Into the subtle air it vanishes.
Sicilians and Trojans dumb-struck stand,
While brave Æneas issues his command:
"The Gods, O Father, by this omen rare
Design that you the diadem shall wear;
While others nobly earned and shall receive
The prizes which with gratitude we give;
Take to thyself, as victor over all,
The laurel wreath and famed Anchises' bowl."
All victors, yet the multitude proclaim
" The prize is his whose arrow caught the flame;"
With one accord to him the prize they yield
Who bore it from the well-contested field.

As then, so now, and through all coming time,
Each grand achievement touches the sublime;
Within each field of learned labor lies,
For all who will contest, a fitting prize;
The higher flight demands the higher aim—
'Tis only these that catch the heavenly flame.

Aiming and striving thus, still aiming high,
Till backward we behold the radiant sky,
Still onward, may we reach the golden way,
The brighter light of an eternal day.

---

## THE DOCTOR'S WOOING.

Oh! do you love me, Mary mine?
  I'd like before we part
To test your soul's affection, and
  To sound your little heart.

Your eyes say yes! My dearest pet,
  Oh! grant me the belief
That I will soothe your sorrow, love,
  And medicine your grief.

We'll tell each other of our love
  As through life's vale we pace;
Lay bare our hearts, and make a di-
  Agnosis of our case.

You'll do the household work; but that
  Hard times we may not see,
The limits of expenditure
  Will be prescribed by me.

And then, when olive branches come,
  Ah! how we shall delight
In teaching all the little ones
  To practice what is right.

Yes, peacefully our lives will pass
    Our girls and boys among.
I'll guard and watch you, dear; but oh!
    Don't show me too much tongue !

                       *—Hornet.*

## THE DITTY OF THE DOCTOR.

### BY DR. E. P. DAVIS.

*Music: The Mermaid.*

There lived a young doctor in a quiet country town,
    And a fine young man was he;
From the college in the city he'd just come down,
    With his brand new medical degree;—
And the old ladies said "h'm, hum;"
    And the young ladies said "oh, my !"
    And the old doctors said "He's a young swell head,
And we'll soon take the shine from his brand new sign,
    And the blood from his frenzied eye."

But the young doctor had such a fine set of tools,
    Such a mild, persuasive grace;
That people came to think the old doctors fools,
    And call him in their place.
He would actively insert his hypodermic squirt,
    When the parson with the colic roared,
And his agony abated, while it never is related
    That he afterwards complained of feeling bored, bored, bored,
That he afterwards complained of feeling bored.

Now there was a certain judge who was opulent and fat,
   And a mighty man was he;
But he had a great obstruction to his water works' production
   Which grieved him exceedingly.
Where the old doctors stuck with their big, big sounds,
   Our hero won gallantly,
For, with proper expedition and the greatest of precision,
   He speedily passed him a small bougie,
He passed him a small bougie.

So the doctor did the judge's daughter wed,
   And lived in prosperity;
He had intimate relations with the country population,
   And flourished mightily;
There were six pairs of twins in that small town
   In the space of two brief years,
And the doctor led the van, for he was a leading man,
   And when the doctor died the ladies all cried
And they pickled him in their tears.
               —*Peoria Medical Monthly.*

## THE DOCTOR'S LIFE.

PROFESSOR I. N. HIMES, M. D.

*Poem read before the Alumni of Cleveland Medical College
in 1875 by its author.*

Slowly, slowly, slowly we oxidize!
Become old and rusty,
Fungoid and musty,
Diminish in size;

Reputation decreases, and self-conceit ceases—
In the morning we're longer and stronger;
Life's burdens, its hod and its mortar,
Press our vertebral disks something shorter:
Cares fret and wear our facial lines incessantly,
Yet doctors grow old rather pleasantly!
One cannot abide at the patient's bedside
A look full of gloom, a look full of doom;
And so to beguile the sick ones to smile
We reef sorrow's folds in our faces right close,
Present the more blandly the bitterer dose;
And thus, in assuming pleased facial expression,
Our brain cells grow to these fixed lines of joy;
Ill thoughts do not thrive — glad thoughts survive —
All life's new comers we hail with the papa's profession,
"A happy event!" whether a girl or a boy.
Training of mind, expression, eye and tongue,
Good deed and kindly word thus keep us young;
While Science, with illuminated page unrolled,
Shows us the art — to placidly grow old.
Promethean teacher whom we love full well,
If there be not with thee perennial youth,
At least fresh thought is in thy gift,
Fresh thought and truth.

Pleasures of him who knows the ways of plants,
Their rootlets, stems, and branchlets, and their flowers.
The sap distilling spirals of their cells,
Hues changing with the sunlight and the hours;
These pleasures are our own — whose minds enlist
No merely social forms of human life—
Who hold in loving inquiry the race
As sacred as to devotee the eucharist.

For, to the true physician, sacred name
Is age and youth, matron and maid;
'Tis his to barrier the breast aflame,
Passion well reined turned mental force instead,
One day with him can have success, defeat;
A battle won; life saved or lost; retreat
Before slow march of foe; a captain he
Contestant with no mortal chivalry.
From foe or ingrate friend we turn for rest
To inspirations of the lettered page,
Covered with emblems reproducing thought;
Turn we as half weaned babe to mother's breast.
In the well shelved alcove how glad to be !
But every day we leave the shady nooks;
Our duties call us in free air; we see
Nature's true commentaries on the books.
Threading the streets in mornings fresh and bright
We harvest crops of smiles from human faces.
In June and May, rain burnished, glad sunlight,
Is very favorable to such growth of graces.

From workward, playward bound, our sisters, brothers,
Some eyes look up so pure, so kind, so sweet,
Free from suspicion of themselves and others,
We inly say a grace before we meet.
Dark eyes look you through,
Grey eyes lift your care,
Blue eyes speak to you;
Tempered steel of soft grey hair
Lends you patience on your way,
And gentle thoughts imbued with truth,
Chestnut brown and gold of youth
Cheer you like the rays of day.

We pass from thronging streets and smiling faces,
Where all the lines have fallen in pleasant places,
To where, beside the couch, pain-scourged fingers
Have wrought a motto while the dull ache lingers.
So reads it, " Suffereth long and envieth not."
If we look close will we not see some blot,
Because the drooping eyelids were not dry?
Or where the pen from anguish turned awry?
Next haps it that our touch is on the bell
Where young life and new hope together dwell,
Where doubled hands are fisting it away,
Eager already to begin the fray.

Oh ! June of roses, deck each spray with bloom;
Art, hew the formful marble to your will.
There is no chiselled statue in the hall
Or sun-fed flower in valley or on hill
That has so much of earth and heaven combined,
The sacred and the sensuous intertwined.
As fair young mother and her bright-eyed babe.
Arms closing upon neck, warm cheeks together laid.
If, after years, the invisible hand of death
Shadows the laughing eyes whose curtains wide
Would catch a ray in the soul's house at eventide;
E'en terror of death's darkness vanisheth.
When words with accents actor never cons
Of mother's tenderness, " Darling, mamma's here."
She speaks, "Mamma's here, darling, do not fear!"
Symphonious with the angelic choir beyond.

Transfiguration heights of science still must show
A Christ, a God of love, a trysting place;
Else in those master hours of overthrow,
Partings of those whose heart-strings form one woof,

There seems no good but that one find a way
To stop the pulse beats, leave the barren sphere —
Survival of the fittest — to a race
That knows no love, nor hope, nor lasting cheer.

Is our next visit to an outcast one—
With life and opportunities near gone?
Ours be the word of grace to point above
And say, we also meritless, that "God is love."

And this is our allegiance to humanity,
To be with it in earnestness and vanity,
In birth, in death, in merry ringing bells,
Or tolling knells;
In life's miscarryings,
In joyful marryings;
To be with them in childhood, youth and gladness,
Their day of strength, or overstrain and madness;
In age's winter flecked with shine and sadness ;
In times of mirth, in times of prayer,
In careless folly, in frugal care;
Where wealth is served from gold, or where the meal
Is made with poverty from common deal,
Where they are like to roses overweighed with rainy blessings,
Or like the low white clover yielding perfume from rude press-
         ings;
In hate, in blows, in lovings, in caressings;
With him who, hand outstretched to pluck fame's flower at last,
After labor, study, travel, clasps Death's scythe edge in his grasp;
With her to whom the message of the lilies is announced,
Who finds that in her motherhood Death's sentence was pro-
         nounced;
'Mid battlefield's grim husbandry in hills of men and horses,
To list a feeble call for help among the corses;

To risk a life that we may be of other lives the wardens,
When plague would drive to shelter in some far Boccaccio's
gardens.

We know all seasons, and both night and day
Are with all persons in both joy and tear,
Whether the uneasy planet shifts aside
To sunshine or to shadows of the year.

We mark the round of change in life and earth,
Flowers wake on hillsides leaning to the sun,
South winds breathe the dead snow to life in drops
Which flashingly in trickling streamlets run.

The white-capped waves, like little Phrygian boys,
Trip playfully before a spanking breeze,
While summer shadows cool the busy walks,
Falling as fruitage from the broad-leaved trees.

The grand elms flutter golden leaves upon the avenue,
The maple prints its fingered forms in darkly crimson hue,
Brown sparrows stoop to broaden out about cold feet warm down,
Or crystal snow flakes under lamps bejewel all the town.

Might we, like Kirtland and good Delamater,
Pass to repose at the full season's close,
Their bodies resting, but whose souls arose
To closer study of the works of the Creator.

Rest, Kirtland's dust! beneath the lilies—
Valley lilies springing pure—
Whose silver bells and diamond dewdrops
Were wealth that could allure.
Hard by Lake Erie murmurs softly,
Or rises into stormy roar,
Its waves their crested line of battle
Renewing with the stubborn shore.

The fir trees keep a watch above thee.
Whispering the winds that near and far
Tell rock and stream and bird and blossom
What place thy sacred ashes are.

But in new realms, where new birth brought thee.
With wider range than sound or sight.
There, more than rock, stream, bird, or blossom
Are in thy circles of delight.

---

## THE STATE'S BEST CITIZEN—THE DOCTOR!

### BY DR. T. U. FLANNER.

*Read at the Banquet given to the Missouri Medical Association by
the Citizens of Carthage, May 19. 1880.*

In every phase of human life
From earliest breath to latest sigh.
'Mid hours of peace and scenes of strife,
When men are born, and when they die.
In cottage, palace, hovel, hall.
On silken couch, or stony ground.
Where sickness, pain, or death may call,
"The State's best citizen, the doctor's" found.

When others flee contagion's breath.
Forgetting earth's most sacred ties.
And safety seek from march of death,
'Mid healthier climes, 'neath cooler skies—
When others shrink from sight of woes.
And shut with horror from their gaze
The sights which only misery knows.
"The State's best citizen, the doctor." stays.

In every way and walk you tread,
The doctor stands your friend and guide;
　And when you languish on your bed
He faithful still is at your side.
　Though weary, worn and bowed with care,
To give relief it still is his,
　And help your heavy burdens bear,
"The State's best citizen, the doctor" is.

　With open heart and cultured mind
In church or state, in field or mart,
　In all good works his hand doth find
He shrinks not from an active part.
　With all who seek by word or deed
To help a brother man to rise,
　Of every nation, every creed,
"The State's best citizen, the doctor," vies.

　He tells you what to eat and drink,
He tells you when to go and where,
　And when to rest, and when to think,
And when to act and when forbear.
　You ask him where and how to build;
You ask him how to run your schools;
　In every trade and every guild
"The State's best citizen, the doctor," rules.

　Beside all this, his life's beset
With ills no other calling knows,
　His round of duties must be met
Though mind and body need repose.
　Whenever sought, by day or night,
'Mid summer storms or winter snows.
　From grateful shade or fireside bright
"The State's best citizen, the doctor," goes.

While others lie beside their wives
In sweet unbroken quiet rest,
   And strength by slumber wooed revives
The body weak and mind opprest,
   There comes a hurried thundering rap
That to its depths his mansion shakes,
   And starting from his first brief nap
"The State's best citizen, the doctor," wakes.

From out his cosy bed he crawls,
And tries in vain to strike a light;
   Then, stumbling o'er the cradle, falls,
When baby screams in hideous fright,
   And wife exclaims in accents mild,
As from the bed she wildly starts,
   "You clumsy lout!" And then half wild
"The State's best citizen, the doctor," starts.

He slowly to the front door hies,
His *robe de nuit* flapped by the breeze,
   And groping round with half oped eyes
Against the rocker barks his knees,
   As off a tack he madly jumps
Against a door he runs his nose,
   And 'mid the nether darkness stumps
"The State's best citizen, the doctor's" toes.

To his inquiries at the door
He hears a fearful story told,
   How ma'am with colic rolls the floor
Or daddie's got an awful cold;
   Or Johnny's got outside a nickel
Or baby's mighty bad with fits,
   And so to get them out of pickle
"The State's best citizen, the doctor gits.

He stops not now the cost to count
Or barter for a coming fee.
   But quick his saddled horse doth mount
And sallies forth the case to see.
   And thus throughout his whole career
He for the good of others lives ;
   To all alike, hope, comfort, cheer
"The State's best citizen, the doctor." gives.

While others then their lineage tell
And of their deeds of prowess boast.
   We round this festive board may well
Affirm the worth of him we toast.
   And pledge each other as we stand
To keep forever bright the link
   That binds us in fraternal bond—
"THE STATE'S BEST CITIZEN, THE DOCTOR." DRINK!

---

## THERAPEUTICS OF THE GRANDFATHERS.

Mr. A he fell sick;
"Go send for the doctor, and be quick."
The doctor comes and with a free good will,
But he never forgets his calomel.

He takes his patient by the hand,
He compliments him as a friend;
He sits awhile his pulse to feel,
And then pulls out his calomel.

He turns around to the patient's wife —
"Have you paper, spoon and knife?
I think your husband would do well
To take a course of calomel."

Then he dealt out these fatal grains,
Every grain to ease a pain.
"Every three hours by the sound of the bell,
Give him a dose of calomel."

The patient now grew worse indeed.
"Go, ride for counsel, ride in speed."
The counsel comes, with a free good will,
To *double* the dose of calomel.

The neighbors all flocked in to see
The dire effects of mercury.
Oh, what is this affects this man?
It's the perfumes of calomel.

"Now, since I must resign my breath,
Pray let me die a natural death,
And you, my friends, I'll bid farewell,
I give up the ghost to calomel."

—*Medical Herald.*

## ANTIPHLOGISTIC TREATMENT.

A humorous picture of the antiphlogistic treatment, written by "the late eccentric Dr. Brennan, of Dublin," quoted by Professor Stokes, of Dublin, in his Lectures on Fevers:

Any patient, when you get him,
First of all be sure to sweat him;
The next day you need not heed him,
But the third day take care to bleed him.
When he's sweated and he's bled,
Then, of course, you'll shave his head;
Clap on five-and-twenty leeches,
Though the first-cost a crown each is.

When to sink he does incline,
Blister legs, and give him wine.
Tell his uncle or his brother
That you'd like to see another—
Yet let nobody approach
But a doctor in a coach;
For a coach does mighty wonders
In concealing doctors' blunders.

When with drugs you well have swilled him,
Tell his friends *the fever* killed him;
All that could be done was done—
The worst you ever saw, but one;
And this is a mighty consolation
In such an awful visitation.
            —*Louisville Medical News.*

---

## A POE-ETIC AGUE.

Once upon an evening bleary,
While I sat me dreaming, dreary,
In the sunshine thinking over
Things that passed in days of yore.
While I nodded, nearly sleeping,
Gently came a something creeping,
Creeping upward from the floor.
"'Tis a cooling breeze," I muttered,
"From the regions 'neath the floor;
Only this, and nothing more."

Ah! distinctly I remember—
It was in that wet November,
When the earth, and every member
Of creation that it bore,
Had for weeks and months been soaking
In the meanest, most provoking,
Foggy rain that, without joking,
We had ever seen before;
So I knew it must be very
Cold and damp beneath the floor—
Very cold beneath the floor.

So I sat me, nearly napping,
In the sunshine, stretching, gaping,
With a feeling quite delighted
With the breezes 'neath the door,
Till I felt me growing colder,
And the stretching waxing bolder,
And myself now feeling older,
Older than I felt before;
Feeling that my joints were stiffer
Than they were in days of yore—
Stiffer than they'd been before.

All along my back the creeping
Soon gave place to rustling, leaping,
As if countless frozen demons
Had concluded to explore
All the cavities—the varmints—
'Twixt me and my nether garments.
Through my boots into the floor;
Then I found myself a shaking,
Gently shaking more and more—
Every moment more and more.

'Twas the ague; and it shook me
Into heavy clothes that took me
Shaking to the kitchen, every
Place, where there was warmth in store;

" As if countless frozen demons
Had concluded to explore
All the cavities — the varmints —
'Twixt me and my nether garments."

Shaking till the china rattled,
Shaking till the morals battled;
Shaking, and, with all my warming,
Feeling colder than before;
Shaking till it had exhausted
All its powers to shake me more;
Till it could not shake me more.

Then it rested till the morrow,
When it came with all the sorrow
That it had the face to borrow,
Shaking, shaking as before.
And from that day in November—
Day which I shall long remember—
It has made diurnal visits,
Shaking, shaking, oh, so sore!
Shaking off my boots, and shaking
Me to bed, if nothing more—
Fully this, if nothing more.

And to-day, the sparrows flitting
Round my cottage see me sitting
Moodily within the sunshine,
Just outside my silent door,
Waiting for the ague, seeming
Like a man for ever dreaming;
And the sunlight on me streaming
Casts no shadow on the floor,
For I am too thin and sallow
To make shadows on the floor;
Naught of shadows any more.

—*Leonard's Medical Journal.*

# MEDICINE.

## THE STETHOSCOPE SONG.

BY DR. OLIVER WENDELL HOLMES.

*A Professional Ballad.*

There was a young man in Boston town,
   He bought him a *stethoscope* nice and new,
All mounted and finished and polished down.
   With an ivory cap and a stopper too.

It happened a spider within did crawl,
   And spun him a web of ample size,
Wherein there chanced one day to fall
   A couple of very imprudent flies.

The first was a bottle-fly, big and blue,
   The second was smaller, and thin and long;
So there was a concert between the two,
   Like an octave flute and a tavern gong.

Now being from Paris but recently,
   This fine young man would show his skill;
And so they gave him, his hand to try,
   A hospital patient extremely ill.

Some said that his *liver* was short of bile,
   And some that his *heart* was over size,
While some kept arguing all the while
   He was crammed with *tubercles* up to his eyes.

This fine young man then up stepped he,
　And all the doctors made a pause:
Said he,—the man must die, you see,
　By the fifty-seventh of Louis' laws.

But since the case is a desperate one,
　To explore his chest it may be well;
For if he should die and it were not done,
　You know the *autopsy* would not tell.

Then out his stethoscope he took,
　And on it placed his curious ear;
*Mon Dieu!* said he, with a knowing look,
　Why here is a sound that's mighty queer!

The *bourdonnement* is very clear,—
　*Amphoric buzzing*, as I'm alive!
Five doctors took their turn to hear;
　*Amphoric buzzing*, said all the five!

There's *empyema* beyond a doubt;
　We'll plunge a *trocar* in his side.
The diagnosis was made out:
　They tapped the patient: so he died.

Now such as hate new fashioned toys
　Began to look extremely glum;
They said that *rattles* were made for boys,
　And vowed that his *buzzing* was all a hum.

There was an old lady had long been sick,
　And what was the matter none did know;
Her pulse was slow, though her tongue was quick;
　To her this knowing youth must go.

So there the nice old lady sat,
   With vials and boxes all in a row;
She asked the young doctor what he was at,
   To thump and tumble her ruffles so.

Now, when the stethoscope came out,
   The flies began to buzz and whiz;—
O ho ! The matter is clear, no doubt;
   An *aneurism* there plainly is.

The *bruit de rape* and the *bruit de scie*
   And the *bruit de diable* are all combined;
How happy Bouillaud would be,
   If he a case like this could find!

Now, when the neighboring doctors found
   A case so rare had been descried,
They every day her ribs did pound
   In squads of twenty; so she died.

Then six young damsels, slight and frail,
   Received this kind young doctor's cares;
They all were getting slim and pale,
   And short of breath on mounting stairs.

They all made rhymes with " sighs" and "skies,"
   And loathed their puddings and buttered rolls.
And dieted, much to their friends' surprise,
   On pickles and pencils and chalk and coals.

So fast their little hearts did bound,
   The frightened insects buzz the more;
So over all their chests he found
   The *rale sifflant*, and *rale sonore*.

He shook his head;—there's grave disease,—
  I greatly fear you all must die;
A slight *post-mortem*, if you please,
  Surviving friends would gratify.

The six young damsels wept aloud,
  Which so prevailed on six young men,
That each his honest love avowed,
  Whereat they all got well again.

This poor young man was all aghast;
  The price of stethoscopes came down;
And so he was reduced at last
  To practice in a country town.

The doctors being very sore,
  A stethoscope they did devise,
That had a rammer to clear the bore,
  With a knob at the end to kill the flies.

Now use your ears, all you that can,
  But don't forget to mind your eyes,
Or you may be cheated like this young man,
  By a couple of silly, abnormal flies.

---

## THE GOUT

When Munden at his house sometime ago,
Warned a large party from his gouty toe,
A heartless fopling drawled a long " Dear me !
I can't imagine what the gout can be."
"Then, boy!" said Joe, with pain-distorted phiz
" I'll give you some idea what it is :—

Suppose your foot fast in a blacksmith's vise,
Then turn the screw, perhaps just once or twice,
Till you the height of agony procure,
That human nature's able to endure,—
The pain of rheumatism, you thus find out:—
Give it another turn, and that's the gout."

—ANON.

"Give it another turn and that's the gout."

## "TO CONSUMPTION."

### BY HENRY KIRKE WHITE.

Gently, most gently on thy victim's head,
  Consumption, lay thine hand!   Let me decay
Like the expiring lamp, unseen, away,
  And softly go to slumber with the dead,
And if 'tis true what holy men have said
  That strains angelic oft foretell the day
Of death to those good men who fall thy prey,
  O! let the aërial music 'round my bed,

Dissolving sad in dying symphony,
   Whisper the solemn warning in mine ear,
That I may bid my loving friends good-bye
   Ere I depart upon my journey drear,
And, smiling faintly on the painful past,
   Compose my decent head, and breathe my last."

## THE LIVER.

*De Jecore Suo Poeta Queritur.*

Liver, liver, little liver,
   Once so light upon my chest;
*Then* I needed not to question
Wherefore comes this indigestion,
   Like a night-mare's nest.

Liver, liver, swelling liver,
   Secret source of many an ill,
Naught can still thy sad commotion,
Blister, lotion, poultice, potion,
   No, nor Cockle's pill.

Liver, liver, swollen liver,
   So the chained Prometheus felt
When the bird of evil omen,
Fattening on his fat abdomen,
   Pecked beneath his belt.

Liver, liver, who'll deliver,
   When the surging bile boils o'er?*
Doctors order (and it's very
Hard) that port, champagne, and sherry
   May refresh and make me merry
   Never, never more.
                     —*Lancet*

* Ita Horatianum illud: "Difficili bile tumet jecur."

## A MODERN CONSULTATION.

### BY DR. E. P. DAVIS.

*Music—" Merry Maiden and Tar."—Pinafore.*

*Doctor.*     You tell me you've an ill-defined sensation,
*Patient.*    Oh wise and learned doctor that you are!
*Doctor.*     Connected with excessive cerebration.
*Patient.*    Oh wonderful diviner that you are!

*Both.*       Oh excessive cerebration;
           Oh ill-defined sensation;
      Oh wonderful diviner that you are!

*Doctor.*     You're the victim of a mild hallucination,
*Patient.*    You astonish me with such prodigious lore!
*Doctor.*     And you have a growing inco-ordination.
*Patient.*    Well, really, have I any trifle more?

*Both.*       Oh the mild hallucination!
           The inco-ordination, the bright irradiation,
      Of such scientific lore!

*Doctor.*     The cortex of your frontal convolutions
           I will now proceed to thoroughly explore;
      And at once I reach intelligent conclusions–
           How sad! your days of happiness are o'er.

*Both.*       Those frontal convolutions, intelligent conclusions.

*Patient*     Oh melancholy tidings!
           That my happiness is o'er.

*Doctor.*     You are suffering from the gradual invasion
           Of a fatal and insinuating spore,
      Whose inevitable, cruel termination,
           Is that you will surely come to be a bore.

*Patient.*    Oh doctor! you alarm me!
          How really can it harm me.
          And can you not forearm me
          Against this deadly spore!

*Doctor.*    You will shortly feel your cranium expanding,
          And great will be the size which it attains;
          And your knowledge will be ever so commanding
          That not a thing unknown to you remains.

*Doctor.*    'Tis the work of the bacillus cerebrosus,
*Patient.*    Why, doctor! seems to me I've heard of that.
*Doctor.*    And the way to antisepticize the creature
          Is for you to wear a brick within your hat.

*Both.*    The bacillus cerebrosus,
          Bacillus cerebrosus,
          This very night we'll put a brick within our hats!
          —*Chicago Medical Journal and Examiner.*

## THE CLINICAL DITTY OF FAIR CLARABEL.

*(Related in Dislocated Rhyme.*

A rich old merchant in the whisky trade,
    Residing in a certain western city,
Fathered an only child, a charming maid
    Aged just eighteen, and counted on as pretty.
Her eyes were brighter than the stars of night,
    Her cheeks were redder, than the rose of June,
Her figure round and plump, her footstep light.
    Her voice so birdlike, never out of tune.

As Clarabel had just left boarding school,
  It may be mentioned with all due propriety
That her fond father, dear old doting fool,
  Insisted that his pet should try society.
So what with theatre, ball, and opera,
  Our heroine put a whole long winter in,
And, on the following spring, her good papa
  Noticed his daughter growing pale and thin.

"So what with theatre, ball and opera
  Our heroine put a whole long winter in."

Spiritus, on seeing such foreboding signs
  As hectic flush and cough so phthisical,
With gaunt emaciation's horrid lines
  Wasting his daughter's rounded beauty physical.
Resolved to have her little lungs percussed
  By some physician of known capacity ;
Knowing at home the fact would be discussed,
  He took her east ; thus showing rare sagacity.

In Philadelphia's precincts settling down
   They put up at a fashionable hotel,
And Clarabel's papa hurried up town
   In search of Dr. X., a well-known swell.
X. duly came, percussed and auscultated
   And then, with all professional gravity,
In a few words his diagnosis stated:
    " Her right lung gone, the left one has a cavity."

"Heavens!" cried Spiritus, "Can this be true?"
   "Yes!" growled the doctor, "Take her to Cape May
And let her bathe in the ocean waters blue.
   Give her cod-liver oil three times a day.
I do not think she'll last until next fall,
   The treatment I've prescribed will suit her best."
He donned his hat, finished his call,
   Sticking the twenty dollars in his vest.

Straight for the seaside Spiritus departed,
   Acting upon great Dr. X.'s advice.
Once at Cape May, our heroine was light-hearted
   Declaring it was "jolly — awful nice."
She would not bathe nor take her liver oil,
   But danced and flirted all the summer through,
Becoming thinner from this kind of toil,
   While her complexion had a waxy hue.

A certain specialist from New York City
   Stopped at the Cape just by mere accident.
Seeing the girl, his heart was filled with pity,
   And forthwith at good Spiritus he went.
He introduced himself as a physician
   Known from Atlantic to Pacific's border.
He said he noticed Clarabel's condition
   And thought she had some feminine disorder.

"My daughter's lungs, are gone; I sadly fear
  I'll soon consign her to the cold, dark tomb,"
Said Spiritus, checking a rising tear.
  "Bosh!" cried the doctor, "it's your daughter's womb.
Her lungs are sound, her cough is sympathetic,
  Depending on the spinal nerve accessory.
I'll place the girl under anæsthetic
  And introduce my patent rubber pessary."

Sweet Clarabel submitted with ill grace,
  And for three days the gutta-percha carried,
And thought the instrument quite out of place,
  And wondered what she'd do, if she was married.
Old Spiritus paid a hundred dollar fee
  Sending it on to New York in a letter.
The pessary was tossed into the sea
  By Clarabel, who, after that, felt better.

Time sped, and autumn came at last,
  The sun was hidden in a golden haze.
At night the musty clouds the sky o'ercast
  And cheerful was the fire's ruddy blaze.
The crowd thinned out, yet still a few
  Lingered beside the ocean's rolling billows,
And danced each night until the hour of two,
  Then sought repose upon soft downy pillows.

Sweet Clarabel grew thinner, weaker, paler,
  Her cough had ceased—she tried to force it.
High was her cheek bone, let us say her malar,
  And e'en the ribs, projected from her corset.
Old Spiritus, worn out and broken-hearted,
  Thought o'er the matter, counting all the cost in,
And on one bright September morning started
  Along with Clarabel for far off Boston.

He called in Z., of Harvard's famous college,
  A learned and an eminent physician,
Who put forth all his diagnostic knowledge,
  Displaying all his well-known erudition.
"It's evident," said Z., that your dear daughter
  Is laboring under chronic Bright's disease;
Look at this specimen of her virgin water,
  Notice its cloudy aspect, if you please.

The doctor then laid down some rules for diet,
  Prescribed a medicine to take by mouth,
Told Spiritus to keep his daughter quiet
  For a few days, then move her farther south.
He said, "She will not live the winter through,
  The case has passed beyond my skill."
Then terminated the little interview
  By carrying off a fifty-dollar bill.

Now Spiritus, o'ercome with dreadful sorrow,
  Mopping his weeping eyes with a bandanna,
Cried, "Clarabel, we'll start for home to-morrow,
  If die you must, why, die in Indiana.
Home of thy happy childhood's sunny days!
  Spot where I earned my first ten dollar note;
Land of corn whisky and malarial haze!
  Dear quinine haunted, lovely Terre Haute!"

Shortly the couple reached their journey's end,
  Down on the Wabash in old Vigo county,
Where Spiritus called in a doctor friend
  Who had lang syne partaken of his bounty.
For forty years had old Bluepill been striving
  To minister to Indiana's ills.
All day and night over the country driving,
  Helping in babies, fighting off the chills.

Old Bluepill scanned sweet Clarabel's pale face,
    And asked the child about a hundred questions.
He noted down the symptoms of her case
    And also made some sensible suggestions.
"You must not dance," he said in accents tender,
    "You need rest, and some bitter iron wine.
Tight lacing's made your waist too slender,
    But, first of all, I'll give you turpentine."

"She held a bottled tape-worm, head and all,
A horrid varmint measuring thirty feet."

"I think those eastern doctors are mistaken.
    Fain would I speak in profane terms!
Just wait until my medicine is taken,
    And then you'll see my diagnosis—worms!"

Within a few days Bluepill had a call
   From Clarabel, who entered, smiling sweet;
She held a bottled tape-worm, head and all,
   A horrid varmint, measuring thirty feet.

Sweet Clarabel is now plump, fair, divine,
   Her beauty's taken on its pristine glory,
Her lungs and kidneys, organs uterine,
   Are all right now—here ends our story.
The moral of this tale is seen,
   Without intent to give offense,
All country doctors are not green,
   And some great men lack common sense.
               —*Cincinnati Lancet and Observer.*

## SONG OF THE TAPE-WORM.

### BY BOB INGERSOLL.

O I am a jolly tape-worm,
   And live in a gallant man,
Who labors day and night for me
   As hard as ever he can.

I gnaw his bowels every day,
   And fill him full of pain,
Till like a burning snake he writhes
   And the sweat runs down like rain.

I lie in his stomach and laugh
   To see him work and eat,
Till he starves his wife and children
   To give a tape-worm meat.

The jaws of my man make music
   That drives me wild with glee,
And I chuckle with joy when I think
   How the good God cares for me.

I am only a worm I know,
   And a worm of low degree,
But I bless the Lord with all my heart
   For making a man for me.

The Lord is very good to me,
   And I thank him all I can;
But after all I must confess
   He's durned hard on my man.
           —*Ohio Medical Recorder.*

## THE ORIGIN OF VACCINATION.

### BY A MEDICO.

*Rem acu Tetigisti—Plautus.*

### I.

"Where are you going, my pretty milkmaid?"
"To see Doctor Jenner," the milkmaid said;
"I have such a cough, and it bothers me so,
I promised Jack Robin for sure that I'd go
For a draught from the doctor to-day."
And she nodded her head with so saucy a smile,
That no one would think, who was looking the while,
That she needed the doctor, his pills or his plaster.
I doubt she could swear that she did, if you asked her,
That sunny, bright morning in May.

## II.

Ah! how little she thought, that unthinking young lass,
While her little pink feet went atrip o'er the grass,
If Jack Robin had not been so true to his fancy,
As to fear the least whisper of harm to his Nancy,
The great loss 'twould have been to us all.
But so it has proved such a number of times
As I have not the space to recount in my rhymes;
Great events have beginnings so small.

## III.

Well! to keep by my milkmaid (as long as I can),
When she'd courtesied her best to the medical man,
And had told (heaven bless her) how badly she felt,
With such pouting red lips, and such ruddy good health
As no doctor could hope to improve;
She sat down to await his compounding her pill,
And their chat led along to the terrible ill
That the small-pox was threatening to prove.

## IV.

Doctor Jenner looked grave, when she mentioned the matter;
He thought it too bad for so careless a chatter;
But saucy young Nancy had nothing to dread,
"But few of the milkmaids would get it," she said,
"For their hands had been sore from the cows,
And altho' it was horrid to milk when the beast
Had her bag all broken out, it was certain, at least,
To keep the small-pox from the house."

## V.

I hope Doctor Jenner that morning in May,
When he finished her pills and then sent her away,

Remembered enough of the lass and the stuff
Not to give her a dose for a cow;
For his mind went far off
From the girl and her cough.

But what does it matter, just now?
For her few simple words, while she waited,
Oh! think with how much they were freighted
When Jenner's quick mind they awakened, to find
How science could conquer the foe,
And gave every nation that blessed *vaccination*
That takes out the sting from the blow.
—*Leonard's Medical Journal.*

## HÆMOPTYSIS.

A sensation of weight and oppression at the chest, sirs;
With tickling at the larynx, which scarcely gives you rest, sirs;
Full hard pulse, salt taste, and tongue very white, sirs;
And blood brought up in coughing, of color very bright, sirs.

> It depends on causes three—the first's exhalation;
> The next a ruptured artery—the third, ulceration.
> In treatment we may bleed, keep the patient cool and
> quiet,

Acid drinks, digitalis, and attend to a mild diet.
Sing hey, sing ho, we do not grieve
When this formidable illness takes its leave.

## HÆMATEMESIS.

Clotted blood is thrown up, in color very black, sirs,
And generally sudden, as it comes up in a crack, sirs.
It's preceded at the stomach by a weighty sensation;
But nothing appears ruptured upon examination.

It differs from the last, by the particles thrown off, sirs,
Being denser, deeper colored, and without a bit of cough, sirs.
In plethoric habits bleed, and some acid draughts pour in, gents,
Sing hey, sing ho; if you think the lesion spacious,
The acetate of lead is found very efficacious.

—*Punch.*

---

## ADDRESS TO THE TOOTHACHE.

### BY ROBERT BURNS.

" My curse upon thy venomed stang,
That shoots my tortured gums alang;
And thro' my lugs gies mony a twang,
      Wi' gnawing vengeance;
Tearing my nerves wi' bitter pang,
      Like racking engines!

When fevers burn or ague freezes,
Rheumatics gnaw, or cholic squeezes;
Our neighbors' sympathy may ease us,
      Wi' pitying moan;
But thee—thou hell o' a' diseases,
      Aye mocks our groan!

Adown my beard the slavers trickle!
I kick the wee stools o'er the mickle,
As round the fire the giglets keckle,
      To see me loup;
While, raving mad, I wish a heckle
      Were in their doup.

O' a' the num'rous human dools,
Ill har'sts, daft bargains, cutty stools,
Or worthy friends rak'd in the mools,
  Sad sight to me !
The tricks o' knaves or fash o' fools,
  Thou bear'st the gree.

Where'er that place be priests ca' hell,
Whence a' the tones o' mis'ry yell,
And ranked plagues their number tell,
  In dreadfu' raw,
Thou, toothache, surely bear'st the bell
  Amang them a';

O thou grim, mischief-making chiel,
That gars the notes of discord squeel,
Till daft mankind aft dance a reel
  In gore a shoe-thick;—
Gie a' the faes o' Scotland's weal
  A towmond's Toothache !

---

# RESUSCITATION OF THE APPARENTLY DROWNED.

This is the plan taught by a man
 In America, much renowned.
To give back breath, and snatch from death
 A body apparently drowned.

Those who are standers by
 Off his wet clothes now must take.
Must rub him very warm and dry.
 And of his clothes a bolster make.

The first step is to make him sick,
  So turn him on his face;
Your roll beneath his stomach stick,
  And the corresponding place
Upon his back press thrice or more;
  Each time you press count four.

The next thing is to make him breathe
  Therefore, turn him round,
Put your roll beneath
  Where the shoulder-blades are found;

Then place his arms above his head,
  Hips between your knees;
Your hands upon his ribs you spread,
  And his sides together squeeze.

With elbows steadied on your hips,
  You sudden forward press;
The weight of your body as it tips
  Will make this labor less.

Backwards and forwards now you go,
Eight or ten times per minute, slow,
At the very least for an hour or so.

If the breathing does come back,
  Let it have its way,
But if it should get too slack,
  Quicken it you may.

When he breathes the standers by,
Who all the time have rubbed him dry,
Put him in the bed they will,
And leave him now to doctor's skill.

                          —*British Medical Journal.*

## HAY ASTHMA.

Maudie Muller, on an August day,
Took the fever called the hay.
Sneezing she went, and her shrill ah-chee !
The mock-bird echoed from his tree.
The judge rode slowly down the lane,
Smoothing his chestnut horse's mane,
And drawing his bridle in the shade,
With a sternutation greeted the maid.
He spoke of the grass and flowers and trees,
The pollen from which makes asthmatics sneeze,
And Maudie forgot her swollen nose
And even her graceful, bare, brown toes.
And listened, while a pleased surprise
Looked from her watering hazel eyes.
At last, with a wild "Ah-chee ! ah-chay !
Ah-choo ! ah-chaw !" he rode away.
Maudie Muller looked and sneezed, "Ah-chee !
That I the judge's bride might be !
He would dress me in silks and diamond rings,
And take me up to the White Mountains.
And I'd use the finest white *mouchoir*,
And never have hay fever thar."
The judge looked back as he climbed the hill,
And heard her sternutations shrill.
"Would she were mine, and I to-day
Were rid of this dab feber of hay !"
Then blowing his nose the judge rode on,
And Maudie was left in the field alone.
Then she took up her burden of life anew,
Sneezing softly, "Ah-chee ! ah-choo !"

Of all sad words of tongue or pen,
The saddest are, "Hay-fever time again !"
Ah ! well for us all that a region lies
Where the infusoria never rise;
And in the hereafter angels may
Find a cure for the fever called the hay.

—*New York World.*

# SURGERY.

## SURGERY vs. MEDICINE.

BY WM. TOD HELMUTH, M. D., NEW YORK CITY.

*Priority in Age and Development Claimed for the Plaintiff.*

I am a surgeon, and in making this assertion
'Tis my apology for doing what I can
To set aside that undeserved aspersion
That says, while medicine is quite as old as man,
Holding within its vast consideration
All wisdom, learning, ethics and decorum,
That surgery is claimed, as is a poor relation,
Being at best "the opprobrium medicorum."

'Tis certainly a subject for humility,
And one 'tis hard for doctors to endure,
That they must own their utter inability
In many cases to effect a cure;
And then, with shrugs and sighs, their patients urge on
To give themselves their only chance for life
By calling on the poor, forgotten surgeon,
Who cuts and cures them with the dreaded knife.

But as for age, I'll prove 'tis all a libel.
(The statement's bold, but I could make it bolder)
For on no less authority than the Bible
I'll prove that surgery is surely older
Than any form of medicine whatsoever;
And having finished, will appeal to the majority
And have the point adjusted here forever,
That "surgery in age can claim priority."

'Tis true, the snake aroused the curiosity,
And gave to Eve the apple fair and bright;
She ate, and with a fatal generosity
Inveigled Adam to a luscious bite.
That from that time disease and suffering came.
Doctors were called upon to cure the evil;
The art of healing, then, with all its fame,
Was at the first developed by the devil.

Medicine thus stands coeval with the sinning
Of mother Eve, fair creature, though quite human,
While noble surgery had its beginning
In paradise before there was a woman.
The facts are patent, and we all agree
'Twas Satan laid on man the direful rod;
That doctors are the devil's progeny,
While surgeons come directly down from God!

For thus we read (although the analgesia
Of Richardson was then entirely unknown)
Adam profoundly slept with anæsthesia,
And from his thorax was removed a bone.
This was the first recorded operation,
(No doctor here dare tell me that I fib!)
And surgery, thus early in creation,
Can claim complete excision of a rib!

But this is nothing to the obligation
The world to surgery must ever own,
When woman, loveliest of the creation,
Grew and developed from that very bone.
Then lovesick swains began inditing sonnets,
And fashion talked with folly by the way,
Then came bulimia for becoming bonnets—
Hereditary epidemic of to-day.

Then, too, began those endless loves and frolics
That poets sing in soft and sweet refrains,
Doctors grew frantic o'er infantile colics,
Announced at midnight with angelic strains.

\*　　　\*　　　\*　　　\*　　　\*

From this the world was peopled, so doctors own,
While you lay claim to such superiority,
That surgery, in the development of bone
As well as age, can clearly claim priority.

My task is done, and with my best endeavor
I have essayed to vindicate my art;
So list my friends, ere friendly ties we sever,
While waning moments bring the hour to part,
Whatever land, whatever clime may hold you,
Some time give honor to the bright scalpel,
And when you recollect what I have told you,
Remember me—'tis all I ask.　Farewell.

---

## STRICTURES.

Lines left on his doctor's table by a patient who was about to start for Niagara Falls, where the water runs down hill, with nothing on earth to hinder it.

---

When sorrow's cloud is cast athwart
　The sunshine of my mind,
When I, with gloomy care distraught,
　No recreation find;
When sighing o'er my hapless lot,
　And what I used to be,
I'll seek some quiet, tranquil spot,
　And pass a small bougie.

Let strictures on my conduct pass:
    Unnoticed let them be:
A stricture somewhere else, alas!
    Is more deplored by me.
In hope this blight on manhood's bloom
    I yet effaced may see,
I'll hie me to my quiet room
    And pass a small bougie."

            —*The Western Lancet.*

Cincinnati, 1857.

---

## THE HONORS THAT AWAIT THE DISCOVERER IN SURGERY.

### BY GEORGE CHISMORE, M. D.

Of the doctors in convention, Surgeon Blank a moment claimed,
While he showed an apparatus and its various points explained,
Which he said he had invented for the cure of a disease
That all other forms of treatment but the knife had failed to
    ease.
When he closed, some seven members in their wisdom rose and
    said
They were each of them delighted with the paper Blank had
    read ;
While it showed the greatest merit, they were still compelled
    to say,
That the malady in question could not be relieved that way.
One averred, in his opinion, 'twould be trifling with a life
To attempt to treat such cases without recourse to the knife,
And one warned his fellow members that the plan was yet un-
    tried,
And one prophesied a failure; others, novelties decried.

So, in short, each poured cold water in the biggest kind of
  streams
On the head of the inventor and his too ambitious schemes;
Winding up with the assertion, that, as now the matter stands,
If successful with the author, it would fail in other hands.

In a year or so thereafter the convention met once more,
And again in proper season Surgeon Blank was on the floor,
This time with numerous patients of his own and others, too,
Proving thus to a conviction every point he claimed was true.
And once more the seven members were on hand in wise array,
And in turn, in the proceedings, each arose and had his say.
All were proud of being fellows of a body Blank adorned,
And they each one begged to mention, that, while other doctors
  scorned—
At the time of the invention when the subject first was
  broached—
They expressed themselves delighted and all doubters had re-
  proached.
It was a glorious triumph our esteemed colleague had won,
But it should not be forgotten that it had before been done.
It was true the operation had most uniformly failed,
But then its vital principles no authority assailed.
And then they quoted Heurteloup and Joseph Emile, Cornay
And Civiale, and Jacobsen, Brodie, Leroy, Mercier;
Proving thus that Blank's invention was invented long ago,
And that certain small improvements were the most that he
  could show;
And even in regard to these, each did contrive in terms
To convey the intimation that Blank had from him the germs.
Such is oft the meed of genius, but it's not the only one;
There's the inward satisfaction of a duty ably done;
And the fame that bides forever for such deeds is still in store,
When detraction's voice is silent, when this fleeting life is o'er.

## AH SIN'S WOUND—THE LATEST REPORT CONCERNING IT.

### BY BENJ. J. BALDWIN, M. D.

Most of your readers have heard of my Chinese case.
And how against Ah Sin I had to brace;
But I must tell how the wound by Nature was mended,
And the Chinaman, doctor and all were blended.
I went back next morning—'twas a dreadfully stormy day—
And behold! there was Ah Sin at his linen working away.
Think of the impudence, as he said, out of the corner of his
    almond eye,
"You tinkie me dead? No, no; niggie no killie me; me nebber
    die."
Said I, "You blink-eyed rascal, you certainly will,
If you don't take to bed and swallow that pill."
Said he, "I takie no medicin' from Mellikay man,
I wantie a DOUBLE-BOWEL doctie from China land."
Then I thought if ever I would be able to get my pay,
And decided that now was the time, I'd dun him right away.
He turned up his nose, and said with a smile,
Somewhat "bland-like" and not without style,
"Not yet, Dockie; I'll see you later; just wait a while."
Then I thought of Bret Harte with his "Chinese peculiar,"
And what a good time he must have had in Mongolia,
For never before had I such a taste
Of "blasted cussedness" in any other race.
At first I thought to imitate the Zulu,
But my peaceful inclination told me it was best to subdue
My passion against this Celestial dummy,
And in some other way procure my money.

So this is the way it stands, as fate would have it:
I am on the credit side, while Ah Sin's on the debit.
Just here I'll say to my beloved Wung-Lungie,
If Ah Sin again gets hurt, he'll have to bring the money;
And of my legal friends I'd like to inquire
If there isn't a law, and if not I'll hire
Some one of them a scheme to invent, or plan,
By which money can be squeezed from a Chinaman.

                     —*Medical Herald.*

## A BONANZA.

### BY WM. TOD HELMUTH, M. D., NEW YORK CITY.

A clever young fellow, a student at law,
Had an indolent swelling come under his jaw;
He took many drugs, still larger it grew,
Till it covered the jaw and the clavicle too;
And, though it received every care and attention,
It much interfered with the act of prehension.
The pain was so great that the man became furious,
But relief came at last when C. M. Mercurius
Arrested the sweating and slackened the thirst,
Then softened the swelling, which very soon burst;
But instead of "the corn," oh, strange to behold,
The tumor discharged quite a lump of pure gold,
Which a dentist had dropped in the gum, while essaying
To plug up a molar, long since decaying.
This morsel of gold, like an amœboid cell,
Worked its way to the surface; how, no one could tell,
But it shows how Dame Nature may sometimes grow bold,
Like most other women, and throw away gold.
The patient's delight can't be told in this stanza,
For he fancied his jaw had become a bonanza.

## THE SONG OF THE SPORES.

When you open your mouth or breathe through your nose,
  I am sure you are all aware, oh!
You take in as many live things at a dose
  As bothered the life of Pharaoh.
      For they float on the tide of the air, air, air;
      They float on the tide of the air.


They dart in and out, and they rush out and in
  With a freedom that makes people stare, oh!
And if any one thinks of incising the skin,
  The vermin are sure to be there, oh!
      For they float, etc.


They assume many forms as they change their abode,
  Some are stout ones, but others are spare, oh!
They are round like a cell, or resemble a rod,
  As they wriggle about in the air, oh!
      For they float, etc.


Some say they are starch, and some say they are soot,
  And they think it's a paltry affair, oh!
To smother such stuff in "carbolic dilute,"
  With the greatest precision and care, oh!
      While they float, etc.


But others believe that such pests are the cause
  Of disease neither little nor rare, oh!
So they kill them with lac, and with spray and with gauze,
  As proclaimed from the clinical chair, oh!
      While they float, etc

So sing to the praise of the wonderful Joe,
 Who controls all the powers of the air, oh!
Laying sporules and germs and epiphytes low,
 As they dance on the stump that is bare, oh!
     For they float in the air. etc.

May the sporicide rise, and with each passing day
 Drench the vermin before they're aware, oh!
With the clear sparkling foam of the murderous spray,
 As they circle about in the air, oh!
     For they float, etc

And may swift-winged time hasten onward in flight,
 Till it joyfully comes to declare, oh!
That the spore-killer ranks as a baronet or knight.[1]
 For exploits in the clinical chair, oh!
     For he kills every germ in the air, air, air,
     He kills every germ in the air.

---

1. This song was written by a student in Edinburgh University in 1872. while Prof. Lister was still in that school and eleven years before the honor of Knighthood was conferred upon him.

# OBSTETRICS.

## THE NEW ARRIVAL.

### MA.

A charming, little, tiddy, iddy bit of mother's bliss;
  A tiny toddles, sweet as flowers of spring;
A precious popsy wopsy — give its mammy, den, a kiss;
  A pretty, darling, itsy, witsy ting!

"My eyes! Is that the baby? What a jolly little pup!"

### PA.

So that's the little fellow! H'm! A healthy-looking chap;
  Another mouth to feed as sure as fate!
No, wife, I *don't* consider that his coming's a mishap.
  But still I *could* have done with less than eight.

### BROTHER.

My eye!   Is that the baby?   What a jolly little pup!
  But I say, ma, wherever is its nose?
And I say, father, by-and-by, when he gets more grown-up,
  He'll wear my worn-out jackets, I suppose?

### UNCLE.

Another?   Well, thank goodness, I am not a married man.
  What!   Don't I think him pretty?   No, I don't.
To keep him from the work-house you must do the best you can;
  Don't think that I'll assist you—for I wont!

### DOCTOR.

How are we getting on to-day?   I trust we soon shall mend.
  We mustn't think we're strong just yet you know;
We'd better take a something, which this afternoon I'll send,
  And let me see — hum! — ha! — ah, yes — just so.

### NURSE.

He's lovely, that he is, mum!  See them sturdy little legs!
  He's twice the size of Mrs. Smithers' third;
And when he comes a-cutting of his little toosy-pegs,
  He'll be a man, he will, upon my word.

### NEIGHBOR.

Oh yes, dear, he *looks* healthy, but you mustn't trust to that—
  I do not wish, of course, your hopes to dash —
But when I see a tender babe, so ruddy, strong, and fat,
  I—look, dear, on his face! Is that a rash?

### MA (*Da capo*).

A charming, little, tiddy, iddy bit of mother's bliss!
  A tiny toddles, sweet as flowers of spring!
A precious popsy wopsy — give its mammy, den, a kiss;
  A pretty, darling, itsy, witsy ting!
             — *Leonard's Medical Journal.*

## A BALLADE OF YE BLUE GLASS.

### Canto I.

A very scientific gent was Doctor Vitreous Browne,
Who practiced his vocation in a certain Eastern town;
A man of brain and culture, with thoughts above a pill,
Famed for his erudition and most audacious s—kill.

Fond of all new ideas was Doctor Vitreous Browne,
Who often rode a hobby, and was apt to ride it down.
When phlebotomy was all the go, it may with truth be said:
The Doctor fiercely shouted, "Blood!" and all his patients bled.

When hypodermics first appeared, 'twas Doctor Vitreous
    Browne
Who purchased an imported one, while with a horrid frown
He used his little morphine punch for curing every pain,
And many a patient fell asleep—and never woke again.

When batteries were introduced, 'twas Doctor Vitreous Browne
Who bought a silver mounted one, paying for it fifty pound,
And, taking every patient out, would confidently tell " 'em"
He'd cure with electricity their softening cerebellum.

But why prolong in fearful and awfully jingling rhymes,
How learned Doctor Vitreous Browne kept even with the times,
Trying every new invention e'er discovered 'neath the sun,
Until finally he landed on rather a Pleasant-on (e)?

For it happened one spring morning, as Doctor Browne arose
From the nightmare dream of glory which lulled his sweet re-
    pose,
That an item in a journal, left daily at his door,
Awaked his curiosity as he perused it o'er.

'Twas this:  "It's been discovered, if rays of sunlight pass
Through the atomic elements of cerulean colored glass,
That, acting on the texture of any living thing,
'Twill cause a century plant to bloom, sick mocking-birds to
    sing."

A joyous smile lit up the face of Doctor Vitreous Browne,
As he gathered up his newspaper, hurried on his dressing-gown;
And at his morning coffee kept wondering more and more
Why he had not thought of this new idea long before.

" 'Twill cure cramp, colic, phthisis, mumps and the bleeding-
    pile,
Cause secretion of the gastric juice, stir up the gentle bile,
Heal cancers, ulcers, fistulas; in fact, we'll now prepare to
Offer it as a panacea for all ills flesh is heir to."

The doctor was delighted as he went reading on
Of those wonderful discoveries of General Pleasanton;
And when at last a sudden exclamation he bestowed,
'Twas, "I'll try on the blue-glass dodge; if I don't I'll be
    blowed!"

## Canto II.

A week has passed, and now behold a transformation new,
The noble doctor seated in a room of azure hue,
Where the drapery, carpets and furniture by the light of the
    windows glow,
A lovely scene of ultramarine, tinted with indigo.

A tap is heard upon the door.  "Come in!" the Doctor says,
Waiting to see his patient with most expectant eyes;
Enter, a silk clad female with waist both long and slender,
Her clothes denoting luxury, her pursed lips legal tender.

"This, I suppose, is Doctor Browne?" The Doctor nodded
 slightly.
"Please take a chair," and, "Please sit down," he added most
 politely.
The lady gazed about the room for moments one or two,
And then she murmured sadly: "Doctor, I am very blue."

Then spoke the worthy doctor: "Madam, if that is all,
Move closer to the window, where cerulean rays do fall;
If you feel blue, I'll cure that symptom up *instanter*
On the principle *"similia similibus curantur."*

Then quoth the lady quickly, with signs of rising wrath:
"It was not my intention, Doctor, to consult a homœopath;
My husband is a pork-packer, and you may rest assured
That, though not very regular, 'I won't be sugar-cured.'

"Listen to my tale of woe, Doctor. Let me pour out my dis-
 tress;
If I had my proper title, I should be a baroness.
Though for fifteen long years married, I, Angeline McCabe,
Have waited all in vain, Doctor, shall I say it?—for a babe."

Then the sympathizing doctor with a blue blush on each cheek,
Controlling his emotions, managed at last to speak.
"O, lady fair, dispel your grief, let all your sorrows pass;
I'll work a miracle for you by means of the blue glass.

Recline upon yon sofa, and let the sunlight play
On your most slender abdomen with its health-giving ray;
'Twill tone up all the organs, strengthen the circulation,
And possibly may add one to a future generation.

"In the meantime I'll leave the room, locking the door behind,
And in the course of half an hour you certainly will find

That very strange phenomena will surely come to pass.
Don't mind your feelings! Shut your eyes! And dream of the
    blue-glass."

The doctor left his patient there for fully half an hour,
And on returning found that she was blooming as a flower;
"Now go right home," he kindly said, "and you be sure to-
    night
To kiss your husband, Angeline, and tell him it's all right.


## Canto III.

Three-quarters of a year have passed, and the entire town
Unite in singing praises of the learned Doctor Browne;
For no such grand and wondrous cure was e'er to mankind given,
Since the episode of Sarah and the miracle of Heaven.

No more shall childless women wander through this vale of
    tears,
Longing for the realization of the hopes of younger years;
For the sunlight's rays of gladness throw their glory over all,
And each threatening matrimonial storm, will end up in a
    squall.

The happiest of mothers, fair Angeline McCabe,
Hums out a sweet-toned lullaby over her lovely babe;
Whose cerulean complexion and orbs of pure sky blue,
Afford a pleasing contrast to its hair of azure hue.

'Twas thought the babe, when first born, would soon give up the
    ghost,
For the very simple reason, that it was cyanosed.
But learned Doctor Vitreous Browne, with a due amount of
    brass
Showed that the baby's color was owing to the glass.

"What matter if the child was blue from toes to top of head,
We much prefer that color to horrid cardinal red."
Such are the words that from the lips of gentlewomen fall,
Who much prefer a baby to nary a babe at all.

And the great discoverer Doctor Browne from his investigation,
Affirms he's found a remedy against foul miscegenation,
He states that colored wenches exposed to a clear light
Will certainly have progeny, said offspring being white."

Now working on this theory, 'twill surely come to pass,
That the complexion of the coming age will all depend on glass.
That the women of the future will be influenced all the while
In their choice of colors by the "very latest style."

Thus for some years the color will most certainly be pink,
Or, if in mourning we are plunged, a color black as ink.
Orange or purple, red or grey will frequently be seen,
And sometimes, like the Irish, we'll be "wearing of the green."

Perhaps some bold American, with patriotic view,
May stripe his lovely baby in red and white and blue.
But no matter to what color the fashionable run,
Let us all join in songs of praise to Browne and Pleasanton.

### LATER.

A horrid tale of calumny floats on the scandalous air,
And causes all the Doctor's friends to curse and tear their hair;
On account of intimations dropped by some libellous clown,
That the little blue-glass baby hath the lineaments of Browne.

*—Cincinnati Lancet and Observer.*

# MISCELLANEOUS POEMS.

## IN THE CHILDREN'S HOSPITAL.

BY TENNYSON.

### I.

"Our doctor had called in another, I never had seen him before,
But he sent a chill to my heart when I saw him come in at the
  door,
Fresh from the surgery schools of France and of other lands—
Harsh red hair, big voice, big chest, big merciless hands!
Wonderful cures he had done, O yes, but they said, too, of him
He was happier in using the knife than in trying to save the
  limb;
And that I can well believe, for he looked so coarse and so red,
I could think he was one of those who would break their jests
  on the dead,
And mangle the living dog that had loved him and fawned at
  his knee—
Drenched with the hellish oorali—that ever such things should
  be!

### II.

Here was a boy—I am sure that some of our children would die
But for the voice of love, and the smile, and the comforting
  eye—
Here was a boy in the ward, every bone seemed out of its place—
Caught in a mill and crushed—it was all but a hopeless case;

And he handled him gently enough, but his voice and his face
    were not kind,

And it was but a hopeless case, he had seen it and made up his
    mind,

And he said to me roughly, "The lad will need little more of
    your care."

"All the more need," I told him, "to seek the Lord Jesus in
    prayer:

They are all his children here, and I pray for them all as my
    own;"

But he turned to me, "Ah, good woman, can prayers set a bro-
    ken bone?"

Then he muttered half to himself, but I know that I heard him
    say,

"All very well—but the good Lord Jesus has had his day."


### III.

Had? Has it come? It has only dawned. It will come by
    and by.

O, how could I serve in the wards if the hope of the world were
    a lie!

How could I bear with the sights and the loathsome smells of
    disease,

But that He said, "Ye do it to me, when ye do it to these"!


### IV.

So he went, and we passed to this ward where the younger chil-
    dren are laid;

Here is the cot of our orphan, our darling, our meek little maid,

Empty you see just now! We have lost her who loved her so
    much—

Patient of pain, tho' as quick as a sensitive plant to the touch:

Hers was the prettiest prattle, it often moved me to tears,

Hers was the gratefulest heart I have found in a child of her
years.

Nay, you remember our Emmie; you used to send her the
flowers;

How she would smile at 'em, play with 'em, talk to 'em, hours
after hours!

They that can wander at will where the works of the Lord are
revealed

Little guess what joy can be got from a cowslip out of a field.

Flowers to these "spirits in prison" are all they can know of the
spring,

They freshen and sweeten the wards like the waft of an angel's
wing;

And she lay with a flower in one hand—in her thin hands crossed
on her breast;

Wan, but as pretty as heart can desire, and we thought her at
rest,

Quietly sleeping—so quiet, our doctor said, "Poor little dear,

Nurse, I must do it to-morrow; she'll never live through it, I
fear."

## V.

I walked with our kindly old doctor as far as the head of the
stair,

Then I returned to the ward; the child didn't see I was there.

## VI.

Never since I was nurse had I been so grieved and so vexed!

Emmie had heard him. Softly she called from her cot to the
next:

"He says I shall never live through it; O, Annie, what shall I
do?"

Annie considered. "If I," said wise little Annie, "was you,

I should cry to the dear Lord Jesus to help me, for, Emmie,
    you see,
It's all in the picture there ; little children should come to me."
Meaning the print that you gave us, (I find that it always can
    please
Our children, the dear Lord Jesus with children about his knees.)
"Yes, and I will," said Emmie, "but then if I call to the Lord,
How should he know that it's me, such a lot of beds in the
    ward ?"
That was a puzzle for Annie.   Again she considered and said:
"Emmie, you put out your arms, and you leave 'em outside on
    the bed—
The Lord has so *much* to see to! but Emmie, you tell it him
    plain,
It's the little girl with her arms lying out on the counterpane."


## VII.

I had sat three nights by the child, I could not watch her for
    four—
My brain had begun to reel—I felt I could do it no more.
That was my sleeping night, but I thought that it never would
    pass;
There was a thunder-clap once, and a clatter of hail on the glass;
And there was a phantom cry that I heard as I tossed about,
The motherless bleat of a lamb in the storm and the darkness
    without;
My sleep was broken beside with dreams of the dreadful knife,
And fears for our delicate Emmie who scarce would escape
    with her life.
Then in the gray of the morning it seemed she stood by me and
    smiled,
And the doctor came at his hour and we went to see to the child.

## VIII.

He had brought his ghastly tools; we believed her asleep again—
Her dear, long, lean little arms lying out on the counterpane.
Say that His day is done! Ah why should we care what they say?
The Lord of the children had heard her, and Emmie had passed
    away."

---

## MARSHAL SAXE AND HIS PHYSICIAN.

### BY HORACE SMITH.

" Fever's the most audacious varlet;
Now in a general's face he shakes
His all-defying fist, and makes
His visage like his jacket—scarlet;
Now o'er surrounding guards he throws
A somersault, and never squeaks,
" An', please your majesty"—but tweaks
The Lord's anointed by the nose.
With his inflammatory finger
(Much like the beater of an urn);
He makes the pulses boil and burn,
Puts fur upon the tongue (not ermine),
And leaves his prey to die or linger,
Just as the doctors may determine.

Though this disorder sometimes seems,
Mild and benignant,
It interferes so with our schemes,
Imparting to our heads a dizziness,
Just when we want them clear for business,
That it may well be termed malignant.

Of these inopportune attacks
One fiercely fell on Marshal Saxe,
Just as his troops had opened trenches
Before a fortress; (what a pity!)
Not only did it make his heart ache
To be condemned to pill, cathartic,
Bolus, and blister, drugs and drenches,
But shocked his military notions
To make him take unwished for potions
Instead of taking, as he wished—the city.

Senac, however, his physician,
Soon gave our invalid permission
To be coached out an easy distance,
First stipulating one condition:
That, whatsoe'er the when and where,
The doctor should be then and there
Lest any syncope, relapse,
Or other unforeseen mishaps,
Should call for medical assistance.

Saxe gives consent with all his heart,
Orders the carriage in a minute—
Whispers the coachman, mounts within it—
Senac the same, and off they start,
Joking, smiling, time beguiling,
In a facetious tete-a-tete—
The subject of their mutual chatter is
Nothing to us; enough to state
That Marshal Saxe at length got out
To reconnoiter a redoubt
Projecting from a range of batteries.

Left in the carriage, our physician
By no means relished his position,
When he discovered they had got
Nearly within half cannon shot;
Wherefore he bawled, with fear half melted,
"For God's sake, move me from this spot!
Doubtless they've noticed our approach,
And, when they recognize your coach
Sha'n't I be fired at, peppered, pelted
(When I can neither fly nor hide)
From some of yonder bristling masses?"
"It's not unlikely," Saxe replied;
"And war I know is not your trade,
So, if you feel the least afraid,
Pull up the glasses!"

## RIP VAN WINKLE, M. D.

### BY OLIVER WENDELL HOLMES, M. D., LL. D.

*An after dinner prescription, at the Massachusetts Medical
Society, several years ago.*

#### CANTO FIRST.

Old Rip Van Winkle had a grandson, Rip,
Of the paternal block a genuine chip;
A lazy, sleepy, curious kind of chap;
He, like his grandsire, took a mighty nap,
Whereof the story I propose to tell
In two brief cantos, if you listen well.

The times were hard when Rip to manhood grew;
They always will be when there's work to do;

He tried at farming—found it rather slow;
And then at teaching—what he didn't know;
Then took to hanging round the tavern bars,
To frequent toddies and long-nine cigars;
Till Dame Van Winkle, out of patience, vexed
With preaching homilies, having for their text
A mop, a broomstick, aught that might avail
To point a moral or adorn a tale
Exclaimed—"I have it! Now then Mr. V!
*He's good for something*—make him an M. D!"

The die was cast; the youngster was content;
They packed his shirts and stockings, and he went.
How hard he studied it were vain to tell—
He drowsed through Wistar, nodded over Bell,
Slept sound with Cooper, snored aloud on Good;
Heard heaps of lectures — doubtless understood —
A constant listener, for he did not fail
To carve his name on every bench and rail.
Months grew to years ; at last he counted three;
And Rip Van Winkle found himself M. D.
Illustrious title! in a gilded frame
He set the sheepskin with his Latin name!
RIPUM VAN WINKLUM, QUEM we — SCIMUS —know
IDONEUM ESSE — to do so and so;
He hired an office; soon its wall displayed
His new diploma and his stock in trade,
A mighty arsenal to subdue disease
Of various names, whereof I mention these:
Lancets and bougies, great and little squirt,
Rhubarb and Senna, Snakeroot, Thoroughwort,
Ant. Tart., Vin., Colch., Pil. Colocynth. and Black Drop,
Tinctures of Opium, Gentian, Henbane, Hop,

Pulv. Ipecacuanhae, which for lack
Of breath to utter, men call Ipecac,
Camphor and Kino, Turpentine, Tolu,
Cubebs, "Copeevy," Vitriol — white and blue,
Fennel and Flaxseed, Slippery Elm and Squill,
And roots of Sassafras and " Sarsap'rill,"
Brandy—for colics—Pinkroot, death on worms—
Valerian, calmer of hysterical squirms,
Musk, Assafœtida, the resinous gum
Named from its odor—well, it does smell some—
Jalap, that works not wisely but too well,
Ten pounds of bark and six of Calomel.

For outward griefs he had an ample store,
Some twenty jars and gallipots, or more;
*Ceratum simplex*—housewives oft compile
The same at home, and call it " wax and ile ;"
*Unguentum Resinosum*—change its name,
The "drawing salve" of many an ancient dame;
*Argenti Nitras*, also Spanish flies,
Whose virtue makes the water-bladders rise—
(Some say that spread upon a toper's skin
They draw no water, only rum or gin)—
Leeches, sweet vermin!  don't they charm the sick ?
And sticking-plaster—how it hates to stick!
*Emplastrum Ferri*—ditto *Picis*, Pitch;
Washes and Powders, Brimstone for the—which,
*Scabies* or *Psora*, is thy chosen name
Since Hahnemann's goosequill scratched thee into fame,
Proved thee the source of every nameless ill,
Whose sole specific is a moonshine pill,
Till saucy Science, with a quiet grin,
Held up the acarus, crawling on a pin!

—Mountains have labored and have brought forth mice:
The Dutchman's theory hatched a brood of—twice
I've well nigh said them—words unfitting quite
For these fair precincts and for ears polite.
The surest foot may chance at last to slip,
And so at length it proved with Dr. Rip,
One full sized bottle stood upon the shelf
Which held the medicine he took himself;
Whate'er the reason, it must be confessed
He filled that bottle oftener than the rest;
What drug it held I don't presume to know —
The gilded label said " Elixir Pro."

One day the doctor found the bottle full,
And, being thirsty, took a vigorous pull,
Put back the " Elixir" where 'twas always found,
And had old Dobbin saddled and brought round.
—You know these old-time rhubarb-colored nags
That carried doctors and their saddle-bags;
Sagacious beasts! they stopped at every place
Where blinds were shut—knew every patient's case—
Looked up and thought—the baby's in a fit—
*That* won't last long—he'll soon be through with it;
But shook their heads before the knockered door
Where some old lady told the story o'er
Whose endless stream of tribulation flows
For gastric griefs and peristaltic woes.

What jack o'lantern led him from his way,
And where it led him, it were hard to say;
Enough that wandering many a weary mile
Through paths the mountain sheep trod single file.

O'ercome by feelings such as patients know
Who dose too freely with "Elixir Pro,"
He tumbled—dismounted, slightly in a heap,
And lay, promiscuous, lapped in balmy sleep.

Night followed night, and day succeeded day,
But snoring still, the slumbering doctor lay.
Poor Dobbin, starving, thought upon his stall,
And straggled homeward, saddle-bags and all:
The village people hunted all around,
But Rip was missing—never could be found.
" Drownded," they guessed;—for more than half a year
The pouts and eels *did* taste uncommon queer:
Some said of apple-brandy—other some
Found a strong flavor of New England rum.

—Why can't a fellow hear the fine things said
About a fellow when a fellow's dead?
The best of doctors—so the press declared—
A public blessing while his life was spared,
True to his country, bounteous to the poor,
In all things temperate, sober, just and pure:
The best of husbands! echoed Mrs. Van,
And set her cap to catch another man.

—So ends this Canto—if it's *quantum suff.*,
We'll just stop here and say we've had enough,
And leave poor Rip to sleep for thirty years:
I'll grind the organ—if you'll lend your ears
To hear my second Canto, after that
We'll send around the monkey with the hat.

### Canto Second.

So thirty years had past—but not a word
In all that time of Rip was ever heard;

The world wagged on—it never does go back—
The widow Van was now the widow Mac—
France was an Empire—Andrew J. was dead,
And Abraham L. was reigning in his stead.
Four murderous years had passed in savage strife,
Yet still the rebel held his bloody knife.
At last one morning—who forgets the day
When, the black cloud of war dissolved away,
The joyous tidings spread o'er land and sea,
Rebellion done for!  Grant has captured Lee!
Up every flagstaff sprang the Stars and Stripes—
Out rushed the Extras wild with mammoth types—
Down went the laborer's hod, the schoolboy's book—
"Hooraw!" he cried—"the rebel army's took!"
Ah! what a time! the folks all mad with joy:
Each fond, pale mother thinking of her boy;
Old gray-haired fathers meeting—Have you heard?
And then a choke—and not another word;
Sisters all smiling—maidens, not less dear,
In trembling poise between a smile and tear;
Poor Bridget thinking how she'll stuff the plums
In that big cake for Johnny when he comes:
Cripples afoot—rheumatics on the jump,
Old girls so loving they could hug the pump.
Guns going bang! from every fort and ship—
They banged so loud at last they wakened Rip.

I spare the picture, how a man appears
Who's been asleep a score or two of years;
You all have seen it to perfection done
By Joe Van Wink—I mean Rip Jefferson.
Well, so it was—old Rip at last came back,
Claimed his old wife—the present widow Mac—

Had his old sign regilded, and began
To practice physic on the same old plan.

Some weeks went by—it was not long to wait—
And "please to call" grew frequent on the slate.
He had, in fact, an ancient mildewed air,
A long grey beard, a plenteous lack of hair—
The musty look that always recommends
Your good old doctor to his ailing friends.
—Talk of your science! after all is said
There's nothing like a bald and shiny head—
Age lends the graces that are sure to please,
Folks want their doctors mouldy, like their cheese.

So Rip began to look at people's tongues
And thump their briskets (called it "sound their lungs")
Brushed up his knowledge smartly as he could,
Read in old Cullen and in Doctor Good.
The town was healthy; for a month or two
He gave the sexton very little work to do.

About the time the dogday heats begin,
Measles and mumps and mulligrubs set in;
With autumn evenings dysentery came,
And dusky typhoid lit his smouldering flame;
The blacksmith ailed—the carpenter was down,
And half the children sickened in the town.
The sexton's face grew shorter than before—
The sexton's wife a brand new bonnet wore—
Things looked quite serious—Death had got a grip
On old and young, in spite of Dr. Rip.

And now the Squire was taken with a chill—
Wife gave "hot drops"—at night an Indian pill;

1. "And, being thirsty, took a vigorous pull."
2. "But snoring still, the slumbering doctor lay."
3. "That's downright murder! cut his throat you mean."
4. "You'll quickly know him by his mildewed air."

Next morning, feverish—bedtime, getting worse,
Out of his head—began to rave and curse;
The doctor sent for—double quick he came:
*Ant. Tart. gran. duo*, and repeat the same

If no *et cetera*. Third day—nothing new;
Percussed his thorax—set him cussing, too—
Lung-fever threatening—something of the sort—
Out with the lancet—let him bleed—a quart—
Ten leeches next—then blister to his side;
Ten grains of calomel—just then he died.

The deacon next required the doctor's care—
Took cold by sitting in a draft of air—
Pains in the back, but what's the matter is
Not quite so clear—wife calls it "rheumatiz."
Rubs back with flannel—gives him something hot—
"Ah!" says the deacon, "that goes nigh the spot."
Next day a rigor—run, my little man,
And say the deacon sends for Dr. Van.
The doctor came—percussion as before,
Thumping and banging till his ribs were sore—
"Right side the flattest"—then more vigorous raps—
Fever—that's certain—pleurisy, perhaps.
A quart of blood will ease the pain, no doubt,
Ten leeches next will help to suck it out,
Then clasp a blister on the painful part—
But first two grains of *antimonium tart*.
Last, with a dose of cleansing calomel
Unload the portal system—that sounds well!

But when the self-same remedies were tried,
As all the village knew the squire had died;

The neighbors hinted this will never do:
He's killed the squire—he'll kill the deacon too."

Now when a doctor's patients are perplexed,
A consultation comes in order next—
You know what that is? In a certain place
Meet certain doctors to discuss a case
And other matters, such as weather, crops,
Potatoes, pumpkins, lager beer and hops.
For what's the use?—there's little to be said.
Nine times in ten your man's as good as dead
At best a talk (the secret to disclose)
Where three men guess, and sometimes one man knows.

The counsel summoned came without delay—
Young doctor Green and shrewd old doctor Gray—
They heard the story—"bleed!" says doctor Green,
"That's downright murder! cut his throat, you mean!
Leeches! the reptiles! why, for pity's sake,
Not try an adder or a rattlesnake?
Blisters! why bless you, they're against the law—
It's rank assault and battery if they draw!

Tartrate of antimony! shade of Luke,
Stomachs turn pale at thought of such rebuke!
The portal system! what's the man about?
Unload your nonsense! calomel's played out!
You've been asleep—you'd better sleep away
Till some one calls you"—

"Stop!" says Dr. Gray.
The story is you slept for thirty years;
With brother Green, I own that it appears
You must have slumbered most amazing sound;
But sleep once more till thirty years come round.

You'll find the lancet in its honored place,
Leeches and blisters rescued from disgrace,
Your drugs redeemed from fashion's passing scorn,
And counted safe to give to babes unborn.

Poor sleepy Rip, M. M. S. S., M. D.,
A puzzled, serious, saddened man was he;
Home from the deacon's house he plodded slow,
And filled one bumper of "elixir pro."
"Good bye," he faltered, Mrs. Van, my dear!
I'm going to sleep, but wake me once a year;
I don't like bleaching in the frost and dew,
I'll take the barn, if all the same to you.
Just once a year—remember, no mistake!
Cry "Rip Van Winkle! Time for you to wake!"
Watch for the week in May when lilacs blow,
For then the doctors meet, and I must go."

—Just once a year the doctor's worthy dame
Goes to the barn and shouts her husband's name
"Come, Rip Van Winkle!" (giving him a shake)
Lilacs in blossom, 'tis the month of May—
The doctor's meeting is this blessed day,
And, come what will, you know I heard you swear
You'd never miss it, but be always there!"

And so it is, as every year comes round,
Old Rip Van Winkle here is always found;
You'll quickly know him by his mildewed air,
The hayseed sprinkled through his scanty hair.
The lichens growing on his rusty suit—
I've seen a toadstool sprouting on his boot—
—Who says I lie? Does any man presume—
Toadstool? No matter, call it a mushroom.

Where is his seat? He moves it every year.
But look, you'll find him—He is always here—
Perhaps you'll track him by a whiff you know—
A certain flavor of "Elixir Pro."

Now, then, I give you—as you seem to think
We can drink healths without a drop to drink—
Health to the mighty sleeper—long live he!
Our brother Rip, M. M. S. S., M. D.!

## A CHEMIST'S VALENTINE.

I love thee, Mary, and thou lovest me.
Our mutual flame is like the affinity
That doth exist between two simple bodies;
I am potassium to thy oxygen;
'Tis little that the holy marriage vow
Shall shortly make us one. That unity
Is, after all, but metaphysical.
Oh! would that I, my Mary, were an acid—
A living acid, thou an alkali,
Endowed with human sense, that, brought together,
We both might coalesce into one salt,
One homogeneous crystal. Oh, that thou
Wert carbon, and myself wert hydrogen!
We would unite to form olefiant gas
Of common coal or naphtha. Would to heaven
That I were phosphorus and thou wert lime
And we of lime composed a phosphuret!
I'd be content to be sulphuric acid,
So that thou might'st soda be. In that case
We'd be Glauber's salts. Wert thou magnesia
Instead, we'd form the salt that's named from Epsom.

Could'st thou potassa be. I aquafortis,
Our happy union should that compound form,
Nitrate of potash—otherwise saltpetre,
And thus, our several natures sweetly blent,

"Oh! would that I, my Mary, were an acid—
A living acid, thou an alkali!"

We'd live and love together until death
Should decompose this fleshy *tertium quid*,
Leaving our souls to all eternity
Amalgamated! Sweet, thy name is Briggs,
And mine is Johnson. Wherefore should not we
Agree to form a Johnsonate of Briggs?
                    —*Michigan University Medical Journal.*

## CUPID AND THE DOCTOR.

TRANSLATED FROM THE FRENCH OF M. GUITARD,
BY E. M. NELSON, M.D., PH.D., ST. LOUIS, MO.

The doctor and the God of love
Serve us both night and day:
  There's the resemblance.
The one is famous in his age,
The one in youth's heyday:
  There's the difference.

They're blind, both of them. yet they both
Investigate with care:
  There's the resemblance.
The one is grave and dressed in black,
The other spry and bare:
  There's the difference.

We make appeal to both of them,
Though dangerous are they both:
  There's the resemblance.
We needs must pay the doctor's fee;
Love paid destroys its worth:
  There's the difference.

Both give to us, within their power,
Yes, life and death are found:
  There's the resemblance.
One wounds us even in healing us;
One charms, but plants a wound:
  There's the difference.

Both of them leave us, hastening, running,
And are—a very little—quacks:
   There's the resemblance.
The one goes when we are right well,
One when life value lacks:
   There's the difference.

"But love has fled my heart, to give
  My doctor place and time."

Despite my four score years and twelve,
As in my youth I rhyme:
   There's the resemblance.
But love has fled my heart, to give
My doctor place and time:
   There's the difference.
              —*The Western.*

## THE METRIC SYSTEM.

### BY A METRICAL MANIAC.

*A Version for the Kindergarten.*

### I.

Hurrah for the meter, the jolly new meter;
Not the long—nor the short—nor the common old meter,
  But partic'lar for you and for me;
'Tis the 10-millionth part from the pole to th' equator,
With it you can measure a township or 'tater,
  A kingdom, a brig or a flea.

### II.

D'ye see this 'ere cube of the tenth of a meter?
That's a liter, to guage how much drink, by St. Peter,
  You can stow in your vast lower hold;
But the gram is the boy to hit up the doctors,
And bother the fogies and gargle-concoctors,
  And make them to blunder and scold.

### III.

O! let them go hang with their ounces and scruples,
Tell the graybeards to "cave" and come down to be pupils,
  Like Ned, Henry, Tom and your Jack;
There's nothing so easy as to learn this nice table;
With Deca and Hecto and Kilo you're able
  To bounce it all off in a crack.

### IV,

The Greek words increase, like Greek brats on the Shannon,
But the Latin decrease, as shot from a cannon
  Looks smaller, the farther it goes;

Haste! Dekagram, Hectogram, Kilogram, heavy,
With Decigram, Centigram, Milligram's levy,
　And gild the bald scalps of your foes.

### V.

Play you're making out bills when you're writing prescriptions,
And your cramped hieroglyphics of th' ancient Egyptians
　Are improved into dollars and cents;
Now what is a gram, or what are the values
Of the devilish and blackguardly weights that we all use
　Annoying the metrical gents?

### VI.

A grain's one six-hundredth of our new gram, boys;
A gram and a third will make, sure I am, boys,
　Your old scruple so base and so mean.
Four grams make a drachm, or at least very nearly,
Thirty-two will fill up the ounce quite as clearly,
　Was anything cuter e'er seen?

### VII.

Then weigh eighty grams of the best old Jamaica
　With a hundred and twenty of water and shake a-
Bout one gram of nutmeg in clean;
　Squeeze in fifteen next of lemon-juice pure,
Shake with ice, and you compound a mixture that's sure
　A babe from its mother to wean.

### VIII.

And we'll drink to the system, the new metric system.
　Who won't take it kindly, be sure we'll assist him,
By sarcasm, by nudge and by gibe,
　If some unlucky fogy with this new appliance
Shall a babe or two poison, you know it is science,
　Continue to weigh and prescribe.

## IX.

Drink again to our system, our superior system;
  For each who will use it, we'll rally and twist him
A garland of chamomile flowers;
  And when every nation has learned this notation
Crime shall vanish and all through creation
  A first-class millennium be ours,

—*Hospital Gazette.*

---

## MEDICAL POMPOSITY, OR THE DOCTOR'S DREAM.

### BY WM. TOD HELMUTH, M. D., NEW YORK CITY.

" Many of them get a fee, will give physic to every one that comes,
when there is no cause."—Heurnius.
" Non missura custem, nisi plena cruoris hirudo."
" The phantasy alone is free, and his commander, reason. — Burton.

---

### PROLOGUE.

Oh ! great Apollo, god of physic, bring
Thy gracious presence near us while we sing
In strains that touch that highly favored art
That first thou deign'st to erring man impart
Fair Juno, too—whose own especial might
Auspicious proved to sacred marriage rite,
O'ershade us now, and ere thou glid'st along,
Drop us one feather to assist our song,
And other spirits hover near, the while,
To aid our effort with approving smile,
While we endeavor in a critic lay
To sing 'bout doctors of the present day.
When Shippen first, for stipulated fees,
Taught physic's laws, and gave men their degrees,

Ten was the number of aspiring youth
Who anxious thirsted for the streams of truth.
Scant was their number, scant the knowledge given,
And scant the patients whom they sent to heaven;
Scant were the mortals whom they cured of ills,
And scant the charges in their yearly bills.
Mankind in days of yore were not so blest
With rheums and aches which moderns so infest.
If ills o'ertook them, they must be endured,
Or tea of herbs the fretting patient cured.
That "iron age," reversing things of old,
Has been converted to an age of gold.
Ten thousand shutters now expose a "tin,"
That tells the world a doctor dwells within;
While countless boys, whose philanthropic mind
Burns with desire to benefit mankind,
Now yearly rush to bow before the shrine
Where dwell the great of Æsculapian line.
Pause—pause, ingenious youth, and let there be
One gleam of common sense 'mid verdancy;
Let not a tinseled stage, with gaudy glare,
Allure your footsteps on—you know not where.
The painted scene looks pleasantly to you,
By light and shade and distance of the view.
Behind 'tis dark, and drear, and damp, and cold,
The cobwebs thick, the ragged canvas old,
The beauteous actress is begrimed with paint—
There's no reality—'tis all a feint.
So 'tis with medicine. Education's stream
Once was so bright that every ladened beam
Of knowledge shone resplendent far and wide,
From college prows that stemmed the rippling tide.

Now, every doctor mans a separate craft—
Crowds it with students thick, both fore and aft—
Becomes a Charon—takes a piece of gold,
Turns knowledge's stream to be the Styx of old,
Cares for naught else than that the cargo yields,
And turns to Pluto's realms the Elysian fields.

Arise, Tarquinius,* from the realms so cold,
Where Nox and Erebus their revels hold,
Shake off their son's, dull Somnus' sway so drear,
And with thy former majesty appear.
Grant us as boon thy dignity's renown,
While we portray some doctors of the town,
Whose bearing grave and keenly glancing eye
Bear witness to their self-sufficiency;
Who shake their sapient locks—look very wise,
Smell at their canes and some new plan devise
To keep the patient ill another day
(Provided, always, that they think he'll pay.)
Talk of the brain, and nerves proceeding thence,
More wise appear, the more they distance sense.
Term pain "neuralgia," or if the man be stout,
Cry out, "Dear sir, you have rheumatic gout."
Tap on the chest—some awful sounds they hear,
Then, satisfied, declare, "the case is clear,"
Draw forth a paper, seize the magic quill,
And write in mystic signs, "cathartic pill."

---

*Tarquinius, surnamed Superbus on account of his great pride and dignity. The same epithet may be applied to so many in the medical profession that it has been thought proper to awake the spirit of the original Tarquin.

## ÆSTHETICS IN MEDICINE.

---

BY E. B. WARD, M.D., LAINGSBURG, MICH.

---

By your leave, I desire just to call your attention,
And will barely suggest that I simply would mention
The fact that the science of beauty is rarely
Brought into physic,—at least not quite fairly!
For men love their lager, and dinners, and wine,
And women, and horses, and everything fine;
But physic goes begging, at least, if not so,
The patient goes begging to let him "go slow."
Now æsthetics most surely and certainly should,
By all that is great and everything good,
Be brought into physic; for what shall we do
With mankind in a fever, "too utterly too?"
And nothing that's lovely, and nothing that's bright,
With a storm coming on and the land out of sight!
In place of the old-fashioned course of emetics,
Why not give a dose of exquisite æsthetics?
Bring your patient to health on a bed of soft roses,
Surrounded by lilies, and sunflowers, and posies!
Now, the knife of the surgeon—as an entering wedge—
Should be shining and bright, with no "feather edge,"
And should penetrate kindly and gently and sure,
With a loving respect for all human gore.
The patient should lie in an easy repose,
With a flower on his breast (a carnation rose),
And be perfectly calm and collected, unruffled,
While gently his sighs by a sunflower are muffled.
Again, when we reach the domain of the eye—
That beautiful organ so like to the sky—

The delicate, sensitive, beautiful slash
Iridectomy calls for, should be done with a gash
So fine in its features, so graceful in curve,
That nature will halt to admire its sweet swerve.
And then—now, you members who do much of this
Will want to get out your old student's hiss—
In the line of obstetrics, where is the face
That never saw loveliness in such a place?
Your patient, of course, is having some pain!
But they're sweet, if they're frequent enough, and again,
They certainly will, and its lovely to know,
Produce a production! a blossom, a blow!
In cases like this there should be no annoy;
The nurse and attendants all pregnant with joy,
Should buoy up the patient (no pun—understand!)
And bring the whole cargo to light and to land.
Again, in prognosing any kind of disease,
It is well to avoid getting up any breeze
By telling the patients they're likely to die,
When the trouble in fact may be all in your eye,
And the patient as safe as old Aristotle,
When he stranded on Greece like a castor oil bottle!
Just tell 'em you'll fetch 'em out all high and dry,
That all things are lovely and the goose hangeth high!
That the bright shining sun will be struck by a comet,
Before the hearse starts, and they ever get on it!
That the lilies which float in the sunlight's broad gleam
Will pull out their roots and start up the stream
Before they e'er launch in Charon's old shell
Which crosses the river and paddles for—well,
Encourage your patients, and teach them to know
That there's something to live for, to blossom and grow;

Don't give up the case 'till flowers cease to bloom,
Because sadness comes o'er you, despondence, and gloom!
Don't take a back seat while blossoms still flutter,
For there's flowers in physic "too utterly utter!"

---

## THE YOUNG LEECH.

[The following piece of poetry of some professional interest is taken from a copy of the "Illuminated Magazine," vol. 2, p. 159, London, edited by Douglas Jerrold. It is signed "Mourant the Monk, Abbey of St. Denis, December, 1843." The book is very scarce, and we have not seen it in print elsewhere]:

Hard by to Londonnes anciente town
    There dwelt a wise young Leech,
Whose conduct for propriety
    Sure, none could e'er impeach.

But well I wot that he was poor,
    And seldom took a fee;
And few and scant the drugs he had
    In his small surgerie.

And though he had but patients few
    To visit and attend,
Yet other patience had he quite
    Enough, you may depend.

It happened then, so says my tale,
    That on a certainne daye
A breathless messenger arrived,
    To summon him awaye.

For two miles off a ladye fair
   Was very ill indeede,
And he must haste to her relief
   With all his utmost speede.

He waited but an instant's space
   His instruments to take;
Then rushing to a neighb'ring stande,
   Thus to a cabmanne spake:

"Now, good cabmanne, I would that thou
   With all thy greatest speede,
Would carrye me to Islingtonne,
   It is a case of neede.

For there in truth a ladye fair
   Is lying very ill,
And I must hurry to her side
   With many a draught and pille.

Now thirty minutes and no more
   Is ample time, I deeme,
For thee to drive to Islingtonne,
   If thou puttest on thy steame.

It is hard by the Holy Church,
   That I do wish to go;
And I will give thee one and six,
   What say thee, Aye or No?

The cabmanne cast one knowinge looke
   Upon the anxious Leech—
"Jump in," he cried, "ere 12 at noon
   Thou shalt the ladye reach.

"A better than my animal
  You seldom ever sawe:
And I this very morning have
  Established a rawe.

"Ere 12 at noon
Thou shalt the ladye reach."

"And though it is two blessed dayes
  Since I have tasted reste,
To do your will, moste gentle sir,
  I'll do my very beste."

Through street and lane their course they took
    With most tremendous speede—
Sure, never since the world beganne,
    Was seen so swift a steede.

Nor was the promise that was made
    A vain and idle boaste;
For as the dial points to twelve,
    The Leech is at his poste,

Now, good cabmanne, thou hast done well,
    For thou thy word hast kept;
The Leech then bade him wait awhile,
    And to his patient stept.

The husband of the ladye fair
    Did give him quick admission,
For to his family he did
    Expect a small addition.

But we must leave the wise young Leech
    To go to the first floor;
And turn unto the cabmanne, who
    Was waiting at the door.

Worn out and weary sure he was,
    As any man neede be;
And how he did comport himself
    I'll tell you presently.

He was humane, and never once
    Did in his duty flagge;
So, turning to his animal,
    He gave him his nosebagge.

One glance toward the clock he took
   And oped the chariot door;
Then sat him down upon the steps,
   And soon was heard to snore.

Meanwhile the Leech, with every care,
   His patient did attende:
And manye a draught of nauseous taste,
   He down her throat did sende.

Hour after hour did he wait,
   And twilight came apace;
But still he stayed to usher in
   Another to our race.

At length, at midnight, through the hall
   A servant quickly hied;
Then oped the door, and one kid glove
   Upon the knocker tied.

And still the cabmanne did him reste,
   Inside the chariot doore;
His head still leant upon his breaste,
   And still was heard to snore.

\*     \*     \*     \*     \*     \*

The sun rose bright at Islingtonne,
   It was a beauteous daye;
And still with his fair patient's lord,
   The young Leech he did staye.

For there they sat in the back roome,
   And they were both right merrie;
For they were quaffing goblets deepe
   Of excellent pale sherrie.

Since midnight had they thus caroused,
  And emptied many a cup;
But now it was half past eleven,
  And the young Leech rose up.

But sure he now did mournful look,
  His brow was marked with care,
For he was turning in his mind
  How he should pay the fare.

The solitary one and six,
  That in his pocket laide,
He knew full well was not enough:
  How could it then be paide?

But to reflect would only serve
  His sorrow to enhance it;
He gave his patient one more look,
  And sallied out to chance it.

And there before his anxious gaze
  The cabmanne sweetly slumbered;
So calm he was, you would have thought
  He with the dead was numbered.

'Twas striking twelve—a sudden thought
  Rushed through the Leech's brain;
He waited till the hour was passed,
  Then called with mighte and maine.

"Up! lazy knave, why sleepest thou?
  Come, take thy one and six;
And mount thy seat, and cut awaye
  Like fifty thousand brix."

But still he slept, and the young Leech
    Did give him many a poke,
Before at last he roused himself,
    And finally awoke.

"Up! lazy knave, why sleepest thou?"

He rubbed his eyes to see the clock,
    As on the step he satte;
Then took the guerdon proffered him
    And humbly touched his hatte.—

"I beg your honor's pardon, but
    I've had no sleep of late;
I just drop't off, because I thought
    That I should have to waite."

As thus he spake, he rose, and took
  The nosebagge from his steede;
Mounted his seat, and urged him on
  With his accustomed speede.

The Leech he smiled a cheerful smile,
  Then gave one parting look:
And well he thought of his own skill,
  As home his way he took.

Meanwhile the poor cabmanne sped on,
  And took his forward way;
Like unto Titus now he was,
  For he had "lost a day."

But little knew he that he had
  Any just cause for sorrow;
He thought that it was still to-daye,
  Nor dreamt it was to-morrow.

But sure I am this wise young Leech,
  Would not have done this sinne,
If he had not been very poore,
  And quite hard up for tinne.

For after that eventful day,
  His practice much increased;
And to find out the cabmanne true,
  I wot he never ceased.

One day, as luck would have it, then,
  The Leech was in the Strande;
And spied his former friend, for he
  Was waiting at the stande.

He quickly told him of the cheat
    That he had play'd that daye,
And into his own service he
    Did take him then straightwaye.

But to this time, though years have passed,
    The cabmanne cannot finde
The reason why he always is
    Thus one whole day behinde.
                    —*Cincinnati Lancet and Clinic.*

---

## LINES TO A DESERTED STUDY.

BY S. WEIR MITCHELL, M. D., PHILADELPHIA, PA.

Hush! feel ye not around us teem
The shapes that haunted Goethe's dream?
When lifted Genius mused apart,
And taste inspired the soul of art,
Young first Love, coy with trembling wings,
And hope, the lark that soaring sings,
And boyhood friendships prone to fade
Through pleasant zones of sun and shade,
With many a phantom born of youth,
The trust in honor, faith and truth
That fails in after years,
The perfect pearls of life's young dream
Dissolved in manhood's tears?
Through Time's swift loom our joys and griefs
In braided strands together run
To weave about this world of ours
Wild tapestries of shade and sun.

And seems it not as if to-night,
Dear, dusty, many-memoried room,
Our souls had lost the threads of light,
And like the eve kept gathering gloom?
Ay, and for one of us the hour
Must have, methinks, a double power,
As backward turns his saddened look,
To view again those many scenes
When life was like an uncut book.
And joy was in her rosy teens.
Yes, even we who later knew
The home of friendship and of taste,
Stand saddened by the parting view
Of scenes by recollection graced.
Ah, there the books looked meekly out
Above an alligator's snout;
And bugs and fossils, birds and bones,
Round-shouldered bottles, jars, and stones,
Stood up in order sage—
Memorials they of every clime,
Remains of every age.
Oh, yes, 'twas here at eventide
We lingered by the table's side,
Whilst Wit her lightning stories told,
And through Havana's clouds of gold
The thunder-storm of laughter rolled,
Till mirth her very contrast brought,
And drooped the brow in earnest thought,
While tranced we sat, as now we sit,
And fast the parting time draws near,
And these stained walls seem gathering grace
As if to grow more doubly dear;

And not an ink-mark on the boards
But wears a half-appealing look.
The mottled wall, the naked floor,
I read them as ye read a book—
As if they something had to say,
And sought but could not find a way;
As often 'mid the waning year,
In brown-cheeked Autumn's bowers,
The leaves ye tread seem rustling low—
"Tread gently, we were flowers."

## THE OLD OAKEN BUCKET.

### BY J. C. BAYLES.

[*As revised and edited by a "Sanitarian."*]

With what anguish of mind I remember my childhood,
   Recalled in the light of a knowledge since gained.
The malarious farm, the wet, fungus-grown wildwood;
   The chills then contracted that since have remained.
The scum-covered duck-pond, the pig-stye close by it,
   The ditch where the sour-smelling house drainage fell;
The damp, shaded dwelling, the foul barn-yard nigh it—
   But worse than all else was that terrible well
And the old oaken bucket, the mold-crusted bucket,
   The moss-covered bucket that hung in the well.

Just think of it! Moss on the vessel that lifted
   The water I drank in the days called to mind,
Ere I knew what professors and scientists gifted
   In the water of wells by analysis find.

The rotting wood fiber, the oxide of iron,
    The algæ, the frog of unusual size,
The water, impure as the verses of Byron,
    Are things I remember with tears in my eyes.

And to tell the sad truth—though I shudder to think it—
    I considered that water uncommonly clear;

"In fact the slop-bucket—that hung in the well."

And often at noon, when I went there to drink it,
    I enjoyed it as much as I now enjoy beer.
How ardent I seized it with hands that were grimy,
    And quick to the mud-covered bottom it fell;

Then soon, with its nitrates and nitrites, and slimy
　　With matter organic, it rose from the well.
O ! had I but realized, in time to avoid them,
　　The dangers that lurked in that pestilent draught,
I'd have tested for organic germs and destroyed them
　　With potassic permanganate ere I had quaffed;
Or perchance I'd have boiled it and afterward strained it
　　Through filters of charcoal and gravel combined,
Or, after distilling, condensed and regained it
　　In potable form, with its filth left behind.

How little I knew of the dread typhoid fever
　　Which lurked in the water I ventured to drink;
But since I've become a devoted believer
　　In the teachings of science, I shudder to think.
And now, far removed from the scenes I'm describing,
　　The story for warning to others I tell,
As memory reverts to my youthful imbibing,
　　And I gag at the thought of that horrible well,
And the old oaken bucket, the fungus-grown bucket—
　　In fact the slop-bucket—that hung in the well.
　　　　　　　　　　　　—*Louisville Medical News.*

---

## SANITARY RHYMES.—THE SKIN.

### BY SIR ALFRED POWER,
*Vice-President of the Local Government Board of Ireland.*

There's a skin without and a skin within,
A covering skin and a lining skin;
But the skin within is the skin without
Doubled inwards, and carried completely throughout.

The palate, nostrils, the windpipe and throat,
Are all of them lined with this inner coat;
Which through every part is made to extend,
Lungs, liver and bowels, from end to end.

The outside skin is a marvellous plan
For exuding the dregs of the flesh of man;
While the inner extracts from the food and air
What is needed the waste in his flesh to repair.

While it goes well with the outside skin,
You may feel pretty sure all's right within;
For if anything puts the inner skin out
Of order, it troubles the skin without.

The doctor, you know, examines your tongue
To see if your stomach or bowels are wrong;
If he feels that your hand is hot and dry,
He is able to tell you the reason why.

Too much brandy, whisky or gin
Is apt to disorder the skin within;
While, if dirty or dry, the skin without
Refuses to let the sweat come out.

Good people all! Have a care of your skin,
Both that without and that within;
To the first you'll give plenty of water and soap,
To the last little else besides water, we'll hope.

But always be very particular where
You get your water, your food and your air;
For if these be tainted or rendered impure,
It will have its effect on the blood—be sure.

The food which will ever for you be the best
Is that you like most, and can soonest digest.
All unripe fruit and decaying flesh
Beware of, and fish that is not very fresh.

Your water, transparent and pure as you think it.
Had better be filtered and boiled ere you drink it,
Unless you know surely that nothing unsound
Can be got to it over or under the ground.

But of all things the most I would have you beware
Of breathing the poison of once breathed air;
When in bed, whether out or at home you be,
Always open your window, and let it go free.

With clothing and exercise keep yourself warm,
And change your clothes quickly if drenched in a storm;
For a cold caught by chilling the outside skin
Flies at once to the delicate lining within.

All of you who thus kindly take care of the skin,
And attend to its wants without and within,
Need never of cholera feel any fears,
And your skin may last you a hundred years.
                    —*Cincinnati Lancet and Observer.*

## PRO BONO PROFESSIONIS.

BY E. B. WARD, M. D., LAINGSBURG, MICH.

'Tis well to be good. but oh! so sad
To be cast in a mould reputed bad,
Without a ray to make one glad,
    In all the desolation!

With tearful sorrow in every eye,
With laughter that longs to breathe a sigh,
And joy that seeks to have a cry,
   To voice its tribulation!

'Tis terrible thus to live and learn,
To feel that your skill most people spurn,
That the masses hope and almost yearn
   To see you come to sorrow!
Yes! to see you work from morn 'till morn,
And come at last in all forlorn,
Out of the little end of the horn,
   Compelled to beg or borrow.

But, so people always have and will
Scoff at your knowledge and spurn your skill,
And say your profession is but to kill
   The patient who is willing.
But still in their hour of sore distress
They're sure to come and meekly confess
Their need of a dollar's worth, or less
   Of your latest mode in killing!

They have used their utmost home-made skill,
Consulted their neighbor's ominous will,
And taken a homœopathic pill
   With some little trepidation.
And still are entirely out of sorts,
Their head feels bad, and their brain cavorts,
Their stomach reels, and their bronchus snorts,
   Like a horse in consternation.

They have swallowed rhubarb by the peck,
Have had a "mustard" upon the neck,
And purged till they feel like a total wreck.

Without alleviation.
Now—if there is anything you can do
To help them out—they'll remember you—
As long as the grass remembers the dew,
　　And no exaggeration!


They'll speak of you to some bosom friend,
Who never had a dollar to spend,
Whose sickly wife you'll have to attend,
　　As partial compensation.
And then by way of a matinee,
They'll ask you to treat their preacher free,
For he's as good as good can be,
　　And worthy your consideration!


And then, with a mild, suggestive frown,
They'll hint at your gently "coming down"
With a suitable sum to help the town,
　　And aid incorporation.
For men who live upon public spoil,
Who never spin and seldom toil,
Should certainly not refuse to oil
　　The wheels of liquidation!


Then you're expected to take a hand
In all reforms throughout the land,
Especially in the temperance band,
　　The only hope of our nation.
For a drunken doctor is worse than bad,
But, catch him sober—they're always glad
To employ him, for it seems so sad
　　To see such profligation!

They love to see a generous soul,
Who acts the busy, bustling role,
And will mingle with them "cheek by jowl,"
    And never take offense.
They want a man they can cuff about,
Pleasant of manner and wondrous stout,
Who is willing to wear his body out
    For love and not for pence.

A man with an easy-going way,
Who lets other people have their say,
And never worries about his pay,
    And doesn't care for a copper.
Oh, yes! but the easy-going man
May stew in the public frying pan,
And work on this noble, generous plan,
    Till he dies a common pauper.

But, leaving the public, we must own
Professional danger grows not alone
In the arid soil and frigid zone
    Of the vulgus populi!
Right in the ranks of professional strife,
A frequent stab, by a skillful knife,
Cuts all the chances out of your life,
    And fits you for the sky!

Or, a cold-blooded wretch, without a spark
Of human love, upsets your barque,
And you are stranded, cold and stark,
    On the rock of consultation,
And left to bleach on a barren shore—
A useless corpse with a sad memoir,
While doctors chant a requiem o'er
    Your perished reputation!

But not alone from the public crew,
Nor yet from professional critics' view,
Come all the troubles destined for you,
　　In the rugged road you travel.
But, away deep in the inner man,
Some little weakness often can
Ruin your prospects—balk your plan,
　　And drop the social gavel.

For instance—take the loquacious chap,
His record is good—he's full of snap,
And his cheek—a thunderbolt might rap
　　And never gain admission;
But people tire of his endless tongue,
And nervous patients get all unstrung
At thought of the song that's still unsung
　　In their enfeebled condition.

Then there's the diffident, silent man,
He stands ahead of the latter clan,
But makes the people guess, if they can,
　　What wisdom he has in store;
Still, here is a point, my youthful friend,
Not a single breath he'll have to spend
To show how much he did not intend
　　To mouth as medical lore.

It is safe to add in a general way,
That the more you think, and the less you say
About any patient, the better play
　　You'll have for your prognosis;
For, the time may come in any case
When unsaid things come right in place,
And never bring upon your face
　　Professional sycosis.

The wiles of woman and all her arts
Should be shunned, for it fearfully smarts
When one of the devil's o'ershot darts
    Strikes a man in the liver.
It interferes with his flow of gall,
And makes him feel most mournfully small,
For the "trail of the serpent is over it all,"
    And it's hard to forgive her!

There's another that I hate to touch,
Because the doctors have said so much
Of consultation with such and such,
    Outside the regular order.
Still. here's the point—don't make a slip
And sell your conscience for half a tip,
"But where you feel your honor grip,
    Let that aye be your border."

Again! Play second to no live man!
Keep up with the times as well as you can,
And never make a flash in the pan
    In shooting at diseases;
For if you do, some lucky drone
Will kill the thing by well flung stone,
And leave you out in the cold alone
    'Till your ammunition freezes!

Once more! Go careful in any case!
Don't hurry the cattle in the chase,
For two to one, in a doubtful race
    The slow horse is the winner!
For while the others are getting sore,
And cutting their quarters in the score,
He's saving his efforts, more and more.
    To give a final spinner.

Lastly: place not your trust in drugs!
They'll kill bacteria and other bugs
If you catch 'em, and put it in their mugs!
  But this is not *de jure!*
Depend upon it, they'll often lack;
But the thing which always stands to the rack,
And always toes the professional crack,
  Is the *vis medicatrix naturæ!*

---

## THE BALLAD OF BACILLUS.

### (DEDICATED TO PROF. VIRCHOW.)

"The same bacillus as that found in hay was produced. On the other
hand, the innocent organism found in hay might by a different method
of cultivation be made to acquire virulent properties. Fed on a vegeta-
ble diet, it was tame and harmless; but, transplanted to another soil and
given animal nourishment, it became savage (verwildert) and virulent.'
—*Virchow's Address before International Medical Congress.*

Oh, merry Bacillus, no wonder you lay
Quiescent and calm when at home in your hay;
You never meant evil in hay-fields no doubt,
Till cruel experiments worried you out.
An innocent germ on a sort of probation,
Oh, why did pathologists try cultivation?

We hear you were harmless and charmingly tame.
So why did our Virchow besmirch your fair fame?
Why should he transplant you, with infinite toil
To new and to wholly unnatural soil?
When food vegetarian kept you so quiet,
Why tempt you to fury on animal diet?

"Verwildert," says Virchow, who surely must know,
You are when transplanted, and cause us much woe;
So prithee, Bacillus, don't travel so far.
You're innocent now and have no wish to ravage,
And we've no desire, dear, to render you savage.

—*Punch.*

## THE NEWCASTLE APOTHECARY.

### BY GEORGE COLMAN, THE YOUNGER.

A man, in many a country town we know,
  Professes openly with death to wrestle;
Entering the field against the grimly foe,
  Armed with a mortar and a pestle.

Yet, some affirm, no enemies they are;
But meet just like prize fighters in a fair,
Who first shake hands before they box,
Then give each other plaguey knocks,
  With all the love and kindness of a brother.
So, many a suffering patient saith,
Though the apothecary fights with death,
  Still, they're sworn friends to one another.

A member of this Æsculapian line
Lived at Newcastle-upon-Tyne;
No man could better gild a pill,
Or make a bill,
  Or mix a draught, or bleed, or blister,
Or draw a tooth out of your head,
Or chatter scandal by your bed,
  Or give a clyster.

Of occupations these were *quantum suff.*
Yet, still, he thought the list not large enough;
   And therefore midwifery he chose to pin to't.
This balanced things, for if he hurl'd
A few score mortals from the world,
   He made amends by bringing others into't.

His fame full six miles 'round the country ran;
   In short, in reputation he was *solus*;
All the old women called him a fine man.
   His name was Bolus.

Benjamin Bolus, though in trade
   (Which oftentimes will genius fetter),
Read works of fancy, it is said,
   And cultivated the belles-lettres.

And why should this be thought so odd?
   Can't men have taste who cure a phthisic?
Of poetry though patron god,
   Apollo patronizes physic.

Bolus loved verse, and took so much delight in't
That his prescriptions he resolved to write in't.

No opportunity he e'er let pass
   Of writing the directions on his labels
   In dapper complets, like Gay's fables,
Or, rather, like the lines in Hudibras.

Apothecary's verse! and where's the treason?
   'Tis simply honest dealing, not a crime;
When patients swallow physic without reason,
   It is but fair to give a little rhyme.

He had a patient lying at death's door,
Some three miles from the town—it might be four—
To whom, one evening, Bolus sent an article
In pharmacy that's called cathartical,
And on the label of the stuff
  He wrote this verse,
Which, one would think, was clear enough,
  And terse:

"When taken
To be well shaken."

Next morning, early, Bolus rose;
And to the patient's house he goes
Upon his pad,
Who a vile trick of stumbling had;
It was, indeed, a very sorry hack;
But that's of course,
For what's expected from a horse
With an apothecary on his back ?
Bolus arrived and gave a doubtful tap,
Between a single and a double rap.

Knocks of this kind
  Are given by gentlemen who teach to dance,
    By fiddlers, and by opera-singers:
One loud, and then a little one behind,
  As if the knocker fell, by chance,
    Out of their fingers.

The servant lets him in with dismal face,
Long as a courtier's out of place—
  Portending some disaster.
John's countenance as rueful looked and grim,
As if th' apothecary had physicked him
  And not his master.

"Well, how's the patient?" Bolus said.
John shook his head.
"Indeed! Hum! Ha! That's very odd!
He took the draught?" John gave a nod.
"Well, how?—what then?—speak out, you dunce!"
"Why, then," says John, "we shook him once."
"Shook him? How?" Bolus stammer'd out.
"We jolted him about."

" 'Why, then,' says John, 'we shook him once.' "

"Zounds! Shake a patient, man!—a shake won't do."
"No, sir, and so we gave him two."
"Two shakes! Od's curse!
'Twould make the patient worse."
"It did so, sir! and so a third we tried."
"Well, and what then?"—"Then, sir, my master died!"

## PRAYER AND MEDICINE.

BY CLAUDE FLORANCE..

A minister stood in his pulpit
   And preached to the people one day,
No matter what trouble was on them,
   If they would only patiently pray,
That everything wrong would be righted.
   This was his doctrine; and then
The choir awoke from their napping
   And grandly responded, "Amen."

But once we were standing and watching
   The minister's wife, sick in bed;
The minister weeping and praying,
   The doctor was bathing her head.
There was wailing and moaning and groaning,
   Her life it seemed creeping away;
Yet the minister, true to his mission,
   Had knelt and continued to pray.

And while they kept on with their praying,
   The doctor kept mixing away,
And pouring down "fixings" and "physics"—
   For doctors ain't much on the "pray."
Well! somehow there wasn't a funeral,
   And maybe 'twas owing to prayer;
But I think they'd have purchased a coffin,
   Had not that physician been there.

            *Atlanta Medical and Surgical Journal.*

# DE ARTE MEDENDI.[1]

## BY D. BETHUNE DUFFIELD, M. D.

Thro' long millenial years our world has swung.
And gloomy Death, with iron hand and tongue
Man's grave has digged, and doleful requiem sung—
"Earth unto earth," "dust back again to dust."
The evil man, the good, the wise, the just,
The tottering child of age, the babe at birth,
Must find alike their rest in Mother Earth.
Death reigns, not only in her caves of gloom and night.
But thro' her open valleys, fair and bright,
For fount of endless youth not yet is found
Amid her rocks, or dells with flowers crowned.

Wise Æschylus,[2] two thousand years agone,
Spoke the one truth this world has ever known:
"Death only of the Gods cares not for gifts;
For him no altar sacrifice uplifts,
Nor hymn of praise from mortal lips ascends,
Since sweet Persuasion ne'er before him bends."
And Seneca, while speaking of the dead
In Christ's own century, sublimely said:
"There's no one but can snatch man's life away,
But none from man grim death can turn or stay;
A thousand gates stand open wide that way."[3]

---

1 Delivered at the Fourteenth Annual Commencement of the Detroit
Medical College, March 2, 1882.

2 Æschylus Frag.

3 "Eripere vitam nemo non homini potest
At nemo mortem mille ad hanc aditus patent."

And so, the wail of pestilential woes
That in the early ages first arose,
Sweeps on in chorus pitiful and low,
Humanity's sad wail, as on its echoes go,
That man is not immortal here below!
Afar in Egypt, men's strong love essayed
Death's crumbling power to check, if not evade,
And by embalming arts, whose secret lay
Hid with the generations of their day,
They sought to hold the body from decay
Till back the spirit came in some far distant day;
While o'er their mummied forms with wondrous skill
They piled the caverned pyramids, which still
Hold fast the blackened visages of kings
Behind the symbol of expanded wings,
And other strange and hieroglyphic things
That hint of far off flights for those hence flown
Within the limitless and deep unknown.
Yet they, who with the surgeon's skilful knife
Opened the veins thro' which this fancied life
(Steeped in sweet spices, frankincense and wine)
Was well embalmed, fled from the temple's shrine
With curses hot pursued and showers of stone
For thus profaning Egypt's flesh and bone;
While down amid the lowest depths of caste,
These early surgeons of the world were past,
The priestly superstitions of the time,
As often since in many another clime,
Held struggling Science then in iron fetters fast.

And so in later Greece the same stern rule
Still held its sway in every new-born school;
Tho' Homer, in his ancient battle-song,
Sings of the healer's deeds in war's wild throng,

And says in words we here may quote again,
"*A healer's worth a hundred other men;*"
Yet brave Hippocrates, whose heart was fired
And with Humanity's own love inspired,
Tho' by the laws dissection of his kind
Was contraband, with penalties assigned,
Discounted Darwin and the Law's red tape
By keen dissection of th' ancestral ape,
And so began the myst'ry to unfold,
Of bones and nerves and muscles manifold
And soon he hazarded the amputation,
Set close the fracture and dislocation,
Ventured beneath the ribs with bloody blade,
And faltered not, tho' friends stood back dismayed;
Cauteries, and cruel moxa with its brand,
And bandaging of wounds with gentle hand,
Were so by him in his dark age displayed,
That he the coming centuries shaped and swayed;
And so to-night, back on the stream of time,
We send a cheer for this Old Man Sublime.

And Rome for full six hundred years or more,
When her grand soldiers daily dripped with gore,
Found no one standing in her martial van
A healing helper of poor stricken man
Till Celsus rose, who, when the soldier bled,
Stript off the battered helmet, bound up the bruised head,
Tied up the ruptured arteries with skill,
And left a name the Ages cherish still.

But lo! the Christian Star ascends the sky,
The world's Great Healer to the world draws nigh,
Walks forth among the smitten ones of Earth,
And by His deeds discloses Heavenly birth.

He healed the lame, the halt, the blind,
And "cast out devils" from the shattered mind;
Bade trembling palsy from the limbs be gone,
Made straight the withered arm and shrunken bone,
And from foul Leprosy's infected cave
Forth drew the men accursed, and cleansing gave;
Then, reaching down the grave, all dark and cold,
He snatched his mouldering friend from Death's stronghold,
And Ages still stand awed at deed so bold.
His skill we see, but whence His mighty power
We know not yet, e'en in Earth's latest hour;
Save that He seemed all Nature's laws to know,
And how to turn their currents' mystic flow
Along the burdened body's crippled form,
And lift the sick to health,
With all its joyous wealth,
The sleeping dead to life, all fresh and warm.
Himself, He humbly styled, "The Son of Man;"
Yet, King of Life was He, ere yet the world began.

Oh, for the day! Say, shall it ever be
This side the fathomless eternity,
That Nature's kingdom with her hidden laws
And all their power with every secret cause
And every undeveloped latent force,
In knowledge ample, from their buried source
Shall be revealed to scientific scan,
As once they were to His, this "Son of Man?"
But with His Star's approach, as by a spell,
From off the feet of Truth the fetters fell;
And onward, onward she was bade to go,
Walking divinely, all the wide world thro'.
And soon fair Science, creeping from her hold,
Grew daily more inquisitive and bold;

And tho' the early church still frowned the while,
And vain Astrology came with her smile,
Still did "the healers" slowly press their way,
And gather wisdom with each new-born day,
Till Alchemy and all her magic arts
And martyr-relics from the Church's marts
And senseless nostrums vanished to the night,
As to the front came Science in her might.

And as the schools arise on Europe's plains,
Fair Science, calmly entering there, explains
To those who turn on her their wondering eyes
The secrets of her new-born mysteries.
Arabia trims her golden lamps to shine;
Then Spain, and France, and Italy conjoin
To throw their light far out upon the world,
And over land and over sea 'tis whirled,
Till grand old England's towers reflect its beams
And a new glory on her banner gleams.

Rudely at first the surgeon there appeared,
As we behold him sketched and high upreared
By poet—first in England's royal line—
Good Master Chaucer, full of wit and wine,
Who more than full five hundred years ago,
When poetry was in its vernal glow,
Paints in his "Pilgrims," the doctor of his time;—
Hark how he gives it in his rough old rhyme—
"With us there was a Doctor of Physike—
In all this world there was not one him like,
To speak of physick and of surgery—
For he was grounded in astronomie—
He watched his pa-ti-ent a full great dele;
In hour es by his magyk natureel,

Well coulde he foretell the ascendent
Of his imayges for his pa-ti-ent;
He knew the cause of every malady,
Were it of hot, or colde, or moiste, or drye,
And where they were engendered, and what humor;
He was a very parfect practisour:
The cause he knew, and of his harm the roote,
Anon he gafe the sicke man his boote.[1]
Full ready had he his apothecaries
To send him drugs and lectuaries,
For each of them made other for to wynne—
Their friendship was not new for to begynne—
Well knew he the olde Esculapius,
And Deyscorides and eek Rufus,
Old Ypocras. Haly and Galyen,
Serapion, Razis, and Avycen,
Averrois, Damascien and Anstotyn,
Bernard and Gatesden, and Gilbertyn;—
Of his diete, measurable was he,
For it was of no superfluitie,
But of great, nourishing and digestible;
His studyes were but litel on the Bible;
In colors red and blue he clad was all,
Lined with taffeta, and with sendal;
And yet he was but easy of dispense.
He keepit that he won in pestilence;
For gold, in phisik, is a cordial,
Therefore, he *lov-ed golde in spe-ci-al*."

And now, a half millenium of years,
I light me down this world of dust and tears.

---

1 Remedy.

And halt in humble village of my birth,
Where gaily sped my early years of mirth;
Full fifty years (or thereabouts) ago,
We had a doctor there—right well I know,
For unto him my *début* into life I owe.
How shall I sketch this lofty, stern old man,
Who handled these first years when life began?
Severe of manner, tall, and dressed in black,
Methodical as Greeley's almanack,
A watch chain pendant, with red cornelian key,
That shone (as oft it dangled down his knee),
Like Mars on lonely Midnight's dusky dress,
Or phosphorescent light in wilderness—
And Phebus! what a hideous, druggy smell
Within his garments there was wont to dwell!
A small apothecary shop I'm sure
Was hidden there; enough "to kill or cure."
I smell it yet thro' all this lapse of years,
Tho' then I smelt it *generally with tears.*
For whatsoe'er our ailments chanced to be,
"Calomel and jalap" was the remedy—
Tho' why this union I could never see,
For if the cal'mel was to stay all down,
And work that fearful purpose, all its own,
Why put the nauseous jalap in the cup,
When that was bound straightway to bring it up?
And were there time, I believe, I'd almost dare
To put this same conundrum to the Chair;
And also this: Why was this doctor always prone
To bleed us ever on the ankle bone,
And in the arm, when we were older grown?
And ample proof have I for all I say:

His scars I carry still,
And doubtless will,
Down to my dying day.
I feel a faintness now, as I recall
The bowl, the lance, the spurt upon the wall,
The ribbon-bandage and that sickening sense of woe

"And drew aside the damask hanging round the bed,
To show a little black-haired sleepy head."

That slowly crept my wounded system through,
And seemed to spread thro' every plaintive toe.
Since naught like this, to-day *our* boys befall,
I wonder why 'twas ever done at all:
As boys we thought it (and 'twas no mean guess)
The very "mystery of ungodliness!"

And yet this same old man was kind and good.
I see him now, as more than once he stood
Within the heavy curtained, silent room,
Laden with pure Farina's choice perfume,
And drew aside the damask hangings round the bed,
To show a little black-haired sleepy head
That lay beneath our wearied mother's eye,
Who smiled upon us with a tender sigh,
As kissing each upon his forehead bowed,
She whispered thro' her lace's snowy cloud,
"The Doctor, boys, last night a present brought,
Which he somewhere among the roses caught,
A little brother for you—now each one come
And kiss him welcome to our own dear home."
Oh, sainted mother, dear mothers of us all,
As we in manly years your pangs recall,
Your patient feebleness, your loving smile,
While near to Death's dark door ye lay the while;
We thank the healer who stood sentinel,
And checked the tolling of the passing knell,
And spared thee till thy work with us was done;—
But now that ye afar to Heaven have flown,
And into holy angel forms have grown,
Look down this night on each surviving son;
Look down in love—and bless us every one!

But here we turn the Past's dull, dingy page
And stand illumined in the present age.
What glories now does happy Science pour
Around the doctor's path and crowded door!
Behold the learned doctor of to-day!
Versed in all knowledge of those schools that sway
The modern mind in Learning's crowded way.

The telephone hangs in his open hall,
Thro' which he promptly speaks to those who call
From towns a hundred miles and more away,
Prescribing pills and potions for the day,
And diagnosing distant babes with croup,
By wheezings heard on telephonic loop;

"God bless the inventors of telephones and sleep."

"Use iodide potasse, or glycerine,
Wet cloths, with streaks of goose grease laid between:"
These are the doctor's words in full direction,
Then bangs the button to cut off "connection:"
And turning to his drowsy wife in bed, He says,

"That babe's all right; they'll grease his throat and head,
To-morrow morning round the floor he'll creep;
God bless the inventors of telephones and sleep."

And what a boon the modern doctor finds
In these new capsules of gum Arabic rinds
The sugar pills—the little and the big—
(Tho' first esteemed a little *infra dig.*),
On ancient styles of dose had got the rig;
And tramps who cure incurable disease,
In order all their customers to please,
Put up bread wads, and many such like simples
In this shrewd form of sugar-coated pimples.
And so cod liver oil, and oil of castor
(So often followed with a swift disaster),
And ipecac, and jalap in a spoon,
Mixed up with currant jelly, jam or prune,
Were straight adjudged unfit for gentle throats,
As assafœtida, or hickr'y pickr'y roots;
When, just in time these ancient drugs to save,
The capsule man appeared and kindly gave
This armor gelatine to-day we see,
And Dr. Bolus now stands *cap-a-pie!*
Why now a dozen doses sly are hid
Within this little shell with gummy lid,
And one of good fat size might carry down
Med'cine enough to cure a country town.
Farewell the stormy strife with boy and spoon,
The mother's peace has come, and not a day too soon;
For if a boy was ere inclined to swear,
And pull his loving mother by the hair,
'Twas when she poured down his reluctant throat
Those drug-shop horrors, on which the doctor wrote,

With cabalistic marks some scrawl like this:
"Signa; misce aquis pluvialis,
Et rec'pe cochl. mag. alternis horis:
Sed dum precatus, bene quassatus."
But all the same, what ere the learned note,
The mix was sure to prove both bane and antidote.

"Ophthalmo-, otoscope and stethoscope
And scopes for every organ known to man."

And then what wonders now our eyes behold!
Strange mechanisms, of curious shape and mould,
That fill the fancy druggists' show case bright,
And set our brains all swimming at the sight,
The various sorts and kinds of microscope.
Ophthalmo-, otoscope, and stethoscope.

And -scopes for every organ known to man,
And twisted tubes, and globes on every plan,
With strange injecting and expelling pumps,
And artificial limbs with cushioned stumps,
And ivory pipes and gutta percha rings,
And, as Hans Breitman says, "all warious kinds of dings."
Such things as no one but a surgeon knows,
With names as long as cross-barred Highland hose.—
I wonder if these doctors, "just for fun,"
Don't sometimes, when their working day is done,
Take hold and with the very best intent
Full "diagnose" each curious instrument.
I'm sure the laymen would like well to see
The learned ones of this fraternity
Take earnest hold of each and every one,
And in succession bravely "try them on,"
That so, as back they laid them on the shelf
Each man would know "just how it was himself."

But time forbids that we should longer stay
In pointing out these wonders of to-day;
And yet there gleams, the wonder of them all,
Bright as the sunny sea round Ocean's wall,
Mercy descending as an angel fair,
With smiles as soft as Summer's gentle air,
To check and soothe Humanity's wild pain
And lull the tortur'd nerves to sleep again.
Oh, Anæsthesia! stern Surgery's fair saint,
Still hear our smitten Earth's distressful plaint,
And come, come ever to the patient's bed,
And sway thy magic wand, and downward shed
Thy gentle, drowsy dew from Lethe's stream,
And lift and bear away the sufferer in a dream—

While Surgery's sharp blade goes flashing down
To regions where abnormal roots have grown,
And lapped and wrapt with cords both flesh and bone.

See yon sad woman, trembling, pale and weak,
Tho' now a blush comes creeping o'er her cheek,
As modestly she draws her dress aside
And yield's the surgeon what she fain would hide,
Her bosom fair, the source in years far flown
Of loving life to children now upgrown;
Their bright young mother's flowing breast,
Where oft she pillowed their frail heads to rest!
But there,
(Alas, that such dread things should ever be),
Yes, there the keen eyed surgeons quickly see
The devil plant has lodged, and vainly tried
Its cursed sprouts and tentacles to hide
In what was once that gentle woman's pride!
She nerves her trembling spirit for the strife
And bloody struggle of the cruel knife,
Lifts up a prayer to those she loves in Heaven,
That strength to her may in this hour be given;
When lo! sweet Anæsthesia appears,
Checks the wild tumult of her fears,
And with a loving hand restrains her tears,
"For pity runneth soon in gentle heart." [1]
And with a sister's sorrow bears a part.

She speaks, reminding her of earlier days,
When she was struggling in that dizzy maze
Wherein brave woman, tho' by torture torn.
Rejoices that her strong man-child is born;

---

1 Chaucer.

And how she once had safely led her thro'
That demon-like, convulsive fever throe,
And anchored her when all the storm was past
Within love's arms, by Home's own cable fast:—
Then bids her rise and with her fly afar
In winged journey to some distant star,
While the good surgeon, does "what he thinks best;"
Then back again to sweet release and rest!
She yields; and Anæsthesia's kerchief white
Drops o'er her face, and now she's on her flight,
While the bright knife, with busy whirl and flash,
Runs its wild round, with bloody thrust and gash,
And lo! 'tis done!
The demon-plant is gone !
And not a scream, or agonizing groan,
Escaped the sleeping form, all strapped and prone.
No, not one troubled sigh or moan !
And as the wandering women earthward come,
Softly descending from the starry dome,
They meet the smiling surgeon's "welcome home !"

God bless the doctor, who can smile away
The patient's tears; and kindly to her say,
" 'Tis over now! I pray you do not weep,
"But lay you down, and drop away to sleep."
"Good deeds thro' heaven," 'tis said, "ring clear, like bells,"
And word is deed, when it dark fear dispels.
And soothing words like these fall soft and sweet,
When they poor, wounded, trembling woman greet;
Sweet as the dew from Heaven's own crystal urns,
And happy he, who their full benediction earns!
For life is sweet to those who love and are beloved,
Death welcomed only when Life's loves are all removed.

Nor does this saint yield only to the call
Of those who dwell in lordly grounds and hall;
She follows marching armies to the field,
And bears the wounded soldier on her shield
From out the battles' roaring storm and flood
To some rude hut or overshadowing wood,
Where the Green Sash essays to stay the tide
That flows from wounds, the Red Sash opened wide.
Brave are the heroes, girt with sash of red,
Who in the battle oft find bloody bed,
But brave as any such that e'er were seen
Are they who serve beneath the sash of green;
Who take war's holocaust within their tent,
And there, with tourniquet and instrument,
And lotion, lint, and liniment,
Staunch the life-flow from shattered trunk or limb,
And put on lips of dying men a hymn—
A hymn of praise for life; when all was dark,
And scarcely visible the vital spark
Within the sinking soldier's drooping eye,
Whose prayer was only that he "quickly die."
But there the surgeon and assistants stand,
A pile of severed limbs on either hand:
And Anesthesia, ever at their side
To check the pain, and staunch the purple tide
On those who lay beneath the surgeon's knife,
And look to him and her alone for life.
Oh, well for them that she is on the field,
Or they of shattering wounds would ne'er be healed;
Well for the hospitals of war and peace,
For war and pestilence will never cease;
Well for the world at large that she appears,
And every suffering mortal soothes and cheers.

Reviving hope and dissipating fear;
And thousand thanks to those who brought her here!
Such names as Warren, Jackson, Morton, Wells,
Will live as long as suffering manhood dwells
Within this weary world of death and funeral knells.

And now, young scientists, to you I turn,
Well knowing how your youthful spirits burn
To pluck the laurel wreath that somewhere blooms
Adown the track of time, but not yet looms
Within your far-off telescopic range
Of things unborn, the curious and strange
Which future years hold fast and unrevealed,
Till you yourselves the casket have unsealed.
Your oath this night, as solemnly it fell
Before this cloud of witnesses, keep well;
Keep bravely well, with all your mind and strength,
In all its parts, through all its breadth and length;
And shield not only sacred motherhood,
But helpless, unborn life, from deeds of blood·
As you would shield a gentle sister's life,
Or guard a brother from the assassin's knife;
And ever let the voiceless babe still find
In you, the God-appointed savior of its kind.

At Learning's shrine still bend the reverent knee,
Disciples now ye are, and long must be,
Children forever in Wisdom's nursery;
For so it is with all who fain would find
The mighty mysteries of her mighty mind.
Yet this you know (as we have seen to-night),
The Past's great tidal wave in power and might
Is here and bears you off in its embrace
To those fair hills crowned with her temples' grace;

A new horizon breaking on your view,
Wide as the one which on Columbus grew,
As near our shores his storm-tost shallop drew.

What, let me ask you, can you yet make plain
Of that dark mystery, the silent brain,
Whose corrugated, complicated folds
In some strange way our active life upholds,
Yet answers not to surgeon's knife or probe,
Tho' deep he thrust them thro' each pulseless lobe?
Were I a painter or a sculptor true,
I know a subject I should lift to view;
The student, in the dark dissecting room
Alone within the candle-lighted gloom,
Pondering above some fellow mortal's brain,
In earnest search to find that subtle chain
Which, catching Life's bright spark from out the sky
And thrilling it thro' pulse and artery,
Kindles to smiles young beauty's lovely face,
Braces the athlete for his panting race,
Wakes in its strength the statesman's mighty power,
Or poet's harp, in his inspired hour;
Gives man not only life, but thoughtful soul,
Till the last hour, when breaks the golden bowl,
And God's eternal silence settles o'er the whole!
There stands the student, pondering, pondering still;
How long think you before my statue will
Give place to him, who glad "Eureka" cries,
And solves this riddle of the earth and skies?
But you, who thro' your coming life must stand
And labor in this shadowy borderland,
Have this and other themes to tax your thought,
As on you toil, and labor in your lot.

The chemist's world behold! how wide its range,
With combinations endless in their change,
That drop their new results with every day,
To help poor sufferers on their weary way,
And show the miner how to draw the gold
Hid in the mountains from the days of old,
And drag the murderer to scaffold stand
By tracking poison to his cruel hand.
'Twas by her flashing arrows, deftly sped,
That grim Astrology fell with the dead,
With all her quips and quirks, and skulls and bones;—
And of her famous "philosophic stones,"
The only one that Modern Science knows,
Or over which a single thought bestows,
Is that gray granite stone at her grave's head;
Of her, "*hic jacet*," is the best word ever said.

And yonder floral world in dewy bloom,
That flings on every breeze its rich perfume,
Invites you to her many buds and flowers;
And by the aid of Chemistry's rare powers;
Bids you distill
Whate'er you will
Of balm or poison from her rosy bowers;
The gates of this new world just now expand,
Go enter in, possess the golden land;
Your Medica Materia enrich,
With no Shaksperean stew of hell-born witch.
But medications rare, and well refined,
To soothe the body and compose the mind;
Perchance some plant may bring to you a cure
For all the woes
And all those torturing throes
That Alcohol's and Opium's slaves endure!

These we expect thro' Chemistry's high art,
And in it you should bear a noble part,
For wealth untold in Nature's bosom lies,
If only sought with cunning hand and eyes.


And tho' in grand old Job's poetic book
(On which no eye irreverent can look)
We read those startling questions put to man,
"Declare! where wast *thou* when this fair world began?
Have Death's grim gates been opened unto thee?
Hast thou e'er entered the deep springs of the sea?
Or in thy hands the glorious day-spring held?
Or all the gloomy doors of death beheld?
Hast thou perceived the dwelling of the light?
Or found the home of darkness and the night?
Can'st thou
The influence sweet of Pleiades ere bind?
Or cast Orion's bands upon the wind?
Know'st thou where Heaven's high ordinance had birth?
Can'st set dominion to it from the earth?
Or lift thy voice up to the clouds of rain,
And call down waters to the thirsty plain?
When all the morning stars together sang,
And Sons of God their lofty chorus rang,
Gird up thy loins, and answer if thou can,
Where wast thou then, O trembling son of man!"


Yet still,
Frail man, in searching out Earth's mystery,
In which lies hid his own high destiny,
Has boldly pushed keen Reason's eye afar;
Far as Alcyone, yon mystic star

That hangs a central pivot strong and high,
Round which revolving worlds go circling by,
Like blazing chariots thro' the starry plain,
And pathless depths of Deity's domain;
But finds not yet in all the heavenly zone
Just where the mighty God has built His throne,
Or where the habitation called "His own!"

But other wonders man has yet to find,
Within that darker world, the world of mind,
Beyond whose cloudy portals you must go
With careful glance, and cautious steps, and slow,
If you its mysteries would solve, and know;—
And so, into that weird and spectral sphere,
Where we are told, our dead ones reappear,
And some stand wondering, while others jeer,
We bid you in your time, to enter here,
And with fair Science and her plummet line,
Sound fearlessly these depths, and bid light shine
Thro' all this shadowy land, that we may see
If truth be there, or only jugglery.
This we should know; for if there be a law
Which from the facts unflinching Truth may draw,
Then publish it to all the earth abroad,
Tho' creeds be shaken and old idols nod;
Truth cannot suffer, for she's born of God.

Thus clad with armor from beyond the skies,
Go forth, as Adam went from Paradise,
Forbid the tree of knowledge—yet still intent
To make the best of his sad banishment,
And thro' all Nature's wide expanse,
To send a keen and penetrating glance,

That he might know all he had power to find
In voiceless nature, that could bless mankind.

Be this your purpose as you say farewell,
And pass beyond your Alma Mater's bell;
Pursue the laws of Truth, where'er they lead,
Tho' roads be rough, and feet may sometimes bleed.
Tho' friends deride, and angry zealots plead;
Who knows but Truth herself, in some near day,
May drop, with folded wing, along your way,
And in your hand the golden key of knowledge lay.

Then struggle on, and on, with all the zeal you can,
Your motto, "Love to God—Love to your fellow-man."

---

## NOEL.

### A CHRISTMAS ANACREONTIC.

Bring me turtle here in bowls!
Bring me turbot, bring me soles!
Turkey, too, and dainty chine,
Balls of sausage-meat combine;
Tipsy-cake and Roman punch;
Of plum-pudding a good hunch,
With mince-pies, both brandy sauced,
Bring—the list I can't exhaust—
Bring them all! and when you do,
Bring the nearest doctor, too!

*—Ohio Medical Recorder.*

## RABELAIS AND HIS LAMPREYS.

### BY HORACE SMITH.

When the eccentric Rabelais was physician
  To Cardinal Lorraine, he sat at dinner
  Beside that gormandizing sinner,
Not like the medical magician,
  Who whisked from Sancho Panza's fauces
  The evanescent meats and sauces;
But, to protect his sacred master
  Against such diet as obstructs
The action of the epigastre,
  O'erloads the biliary ducts,
The peristaltic motion crosses,
And puzzles the digestive process.

The Cardinal, one hungry day,
  First having with his eyes consumed
  Some lampreys that before him fumed.
Had plunged his fork into the prey,
When Rabelais gravely shook his head,
  Tapped on his plate three times and said—
"Pah! Hard digestion! hard digestion!"
  And his bile-dreading Eminence,
  Though sorely tempted, had the sense
To send it off without a question.

"Hip! Hullo! bring the lampreys here!"
  Cried Rabelais, as the dish he snatched;
And, gobbling up the dainty cheer,
  The whole was instantly despatched.

Reddened with vain attempt at stifling
    At once his wrath and appetite,
His patron cried, "Your conduct's rude,
This is no subject, sir, for trifling;
    How dare you designate this food
    As indigestible and crude,
Then swallow it before my sight?"

Quoth Rabelais, "It may soon be shown
    That I don't merit this rebuff:
I tapped the *plate*, and that you'll own
    Is indigestible enough;
But as to this unlucky fish
    With you so strangely out of favor,
Not only 'tis a wholesome dish,
    But one of most delicious flavor!"

---

## A MICROSCOPIC SERENADE.

### BY JACOB F. HENRICI.

O come, my love, and seek with me
    A realm by grosser eye unseen,
Where fairy forms will welcome thee,
    And dainty creatures hail thee queen.
In silent pools the tube I'll ply,
    Where the green conferva-threads lie curled,
And proudly bring to thy bright eye
    The trophies of the protist world.

We'll rouse the stentor from his lair,
    And gaze into the cyclops' eye;
In chara and nitella hair
    The protoplasmic stream descry,

Forever waving to and fro
   With faint molecular melody;
And curious rotifers I'll show,
   And graceful vorticellidæ.

Where mellicertæ ply their craft
   We'll watch the playful water-bear
And no envenomed hydra's shaft
   Shall mar our peaceful pleasure there;
But while we whisper love's sweet tale
   We'll trace, with sympathetic art.
Within the embryonic snail
   The growing rudimental heart.

Where rolls the volvox sphere of green,
   And plastids move in Brownian dance—
If, wandering 'mid that gentle scene,
   Two fond amœbæ shall perchance
Be changed to one beneath our sight
   By process of biocrasis,
We'll recognize with rare delight
   A type of our prospective bliss.

O dearer thou by far to me
   In thy sweet maidenly estate.
Than any seventy-fifth could be,
   Of aperture however great!
Come, go with me, and we will stray
   Through realm by grosser eye unseen,
Where protophytes shall homage pay
   And protozoa hail thee queen.

                 —*Scribner's Monthly.*

## KINDRED QUACKS.

### PUNCH.

I overheard two matrons grave, allied by close affinity
(The name of one was Physic, the other's was Divinity)
As they put their groans together, both so doleful and lugu-
    brious.
Says Physic: "To unload the heart of grief, Ma'am, is salubri-
    ous;

Here am I, at my time of life, in this year of our deliverance,
My age gives me a right to look for some esteem and reverence,
But, ma'am, I feel it is too true—what everybody says to me—
Too many of my children are a shame and a disgrace to me."

"Ah!" says Divinity, "My heart can suffer with another, ma'am;
I'm sure I can well understand your feelings as a mother, ma'am;
I've some, as well, no doubt but what you're perfectly aware
    on't, ma'am,
Whose doings bring derision and discredit on their parent,
    ma'am."

"There are boys of mine," says Physic, "ma'am, such silly fan-
    cies nourishing,
As curing gout and stomach ache by pawing and by flourishing."
"Well," says Divinity, "I've those that teach that Heaven's
    beatitudes,
Are to be earned by postures, genuflexions, bows and attitudes."

"My good-for-nothing sons," says Physic, "some have turned
    hydropathists,
Some taken up with mesmerism, or joined the homeopathists."

"Mine," says Divinity, "pursue a system of gimcrackery,
Called Puseyism, a pack of stuff, and quite as arrant quackery."

Says Physic, "Mine have sleep-walkers, pretending through
  the hide of you
To look, although their eyes are shut, and tell you what's inside of you."

"'Mine are trifling with diseases, ma'am,' says Physic, 'not attacking
  them.'"

"Ah," says Divinity, "so mine, with quibbling and with cavil-
  ling,
Would have you, ma'am, to blind yourself to see the road to
  travel in."

"Mine," Physic says, "have quite renounced their good old pills
    and potions, ma'am,
For doses of a billionth of a grain and such wild notions,
    ma'am."
"So," says Divinity, "have mine left wholesome exhortation,
    ma'am.
For credence tables, reredoses, rood-lofts, and maceration,
    ma'am."


"But hospitals," says Physic, "my misguided boys are founding,
    ma'am."
"Well," says Divinity, "of mine the chapels are abounding,
    ma'am."
"Mine are trifling with diseases, ma'am," says Physic, "not at-
    tacking them."
"Mine," says Divinity, "instead of curing souls are quacking
    them."


"Ah, ma'am," says Physic, "I'm to blame, I fear, for these ab-
    surdities."
"That's my fear, too," Divinity says, "ma'am, upon my word
    it is."


Says Physic, "Fees not science, have been far too much my
    wishes, ma'am."
"Truth," says Divinity. "I've loved much less than loaves and
    fishes, ma'am."
Says each to each, "We're simpletons, or sad deceivers, some of
    us;
And I am sure, ma'am, I don't know whatever will become
    of us."

## THE FOUNDLING OF SHOREDITCH.

### W. MAKEPEACE THACKERAY.

Come all ye Christian people and listen to my tail,
It's all about a Doctor was travelling by the rail,
By the H'eastern Counties Railway (vich the shares don't desire),
From Ixworth town in Suffolk, vich his name did not transpire.

A travelling from Bury this doctor was employed
With a gentleman, a friend of his, vich his name was Captain
        Lloyd,
And on reaching Mark's Tey Station, that is next beyond Col-
        chest-
Er, a lady entered into them most elegantly dressed.

She entered into the carriage all with a tottering step,
And a pooty little baby upon her bussum slep;
The gentlemen received her with kindness and siwillity,
Pitying this lady for her illness and debillaty.

She had a first-class ticket, this lovely lady said,
Because it was so lonesome she took a seck'nd instead,
Better to travel by seck'nd class than sit alone in the fust,
And the pooty little baby upon her breast she nussed.

A seein' of her cryin' and shiverin' and pail
To her spoke this surgin, the 'Ero of my tail;
Says'ee, "you look unwell, ma'am, I'll 'elp you if I can,
And you may tell your case to me, for I'm a meddicle man.

"Thank you, sir," the lady said, "I only look so pale
Because I ain't accustomed to travelling on the rale,
I shall be better presnly, when I've 'ad some rest;"
And that pooty little baby she squeeged it to her breast.

So in conversation the journey they beguiled,
Capting Lloyd, the medical man and the lady and her child.
Till the warious stations along the line was passed,
For even the H'eastern Counties' trains must come in at last.

When at Shoreditch terminus at lenth stopped the train.
This kind meddicle gentleman proposed his aid again.
"Thank you, sir," the lady said, "for your kyindness dear:
My carridge and my 'osses is probbibly come here."

Will you hold this baby please, vilst I step out and see?"
The Doctor was a family man: "That I will." says he.
Then the little child she kist, kist it very gently,
Vich was sucking his little fist, sleeping innocently.

With a sigh from her 'art, as though she would 'ave bust it,
Then she gave the Doctor the child, wery kind he nust it:
Hup then the lady jumped hoff the bench she sat from
Tumbled down the carridge steps and ran along the platform.

Vile hall the other passengers vent upon their vays;
The Capting and the Doctor sat there in a maze;
Some vent in a Homminibus, some vent in a cabby,
The Capting and the Doctor vaited with the babby.

There they sat a looking queer for an hour or more,
But their feller passinger neather on 'em sore;
Never, never back again did that lady come
To that pooty sleeping hinfant a suckin' of his thum!

## PARR'S LIFE PILLS.

POEMS OF BON GAULTIER.

'Twas in the town of Lubeck,
  A hundred years ago,
An old man walked into the church,
  With beard as white as snow;
Yet were his cheeks not wrinkled,
  Nor dim his eagle eye;
There's many a knight that steps the street
Might wonder should he chance to meet
  That man erect and high.

When silenced was the organ,
  And hushed the vesper loud,
The sacristan approached the sire,
  And drew him from the crowd.
There's something in thy visage
  On which I dare not look,
And when I rang the passing bell,
A tremor that I may not tell
  My very vitals shook.

Who art thou, awful stranger?
  Our ancient annals say,
That twice two hundred years ago
  Another passed this way,
Like thee in face and feature;
  And, if the tale be true,
'Tis writ that in this very year
Again the stranger shall appear;
  Art thou the Wandering Jew?

"The Wandering Jew, thou dotard!"
  The wondrous phantom cried:
"Tis several centuries ago
  Since that poor stripling died;
He would not use my nostrums,
  See, shaveling, here they are!
These put to flight all human ills,
These conquer death, unfailing pills;
  And I'm the inventor PARR!"

## A FREAK OF NATURE.

When the doctor saves a life, we appreciate his skill!
But appreciations vanish when he presents his bill.
Though bills of other business men are paid without delay,
When once a year the doctor comes, we tell him "not to-day."
We have the money with us and can pay as well as not,
But the bill goes in our pocket, where it is soon forgot.
Why is it we expect so much from men so free to give,
Forgetting they are mortal, and like us must eat and live?
—*Miss. Valley Medical Monthly.*

## TO DOCTOR EMPIRIC.

### BY BEN. JONSON.

When men a dangerous disease did escape
Of old they gave a cock to Æsculape;
Let me give two, that doubly am got free;
From my disease's danger, and *from thee!*

## MEDICAL STUDENT'S EPITAPH UPON A CAT.

Here lies in her bed longitudinous
The mother of kits multitudinous.
Her life—a perspicuous history;
Her death—an insuperable mystery,
With causes profound and specific
To puzzle the unscientific.
If her rustic physicians—odd rot 'em!
Had given poor puss a post-mortem,
Who knows but the innocent cusses
Might have found that she died of pertussis:
Or haply of intussusception,
The result of too frequent conception;
Or a uterine subinvolution,
Of abortion the fitting conclusion?
It may have been struma or phthisis,
Or coma, asphyxia, emesis;
Or mayhap a stone in her bladder was
The agent that made her cadaverous.
But enough for her fatal pathology—
She made a success of biology;
And if she was weak in psychology,
We stop not to offer apology,
But resign her cold clay to geology.
Sleep, mother of kits multitudinous,
In peace in thy bed longitudinous.
We joy in thy prolific history;
We mourn thy cadaverous mystery.

## THE DOCTOR'S DREAM.

BY W. S. BATTLES, M. D.

*Delivered before the Alumni of Starling Medical College.*

I moved, and could not feel my limbs,
   I was so light almost
I thought that I had died in sleep,
   And was a blessed ghost.
           —*Coleridge's Ancient Mariner.*

I had a dream, and in that dream
   I thought that I had passed
Into that realm of blissful rest
   The doctors reach at last.

I dreamed of all the ups and downs
   Of thirty years of practice,
That brought with many a scented rose,
   Its compensating cactus.

I thought of all the praise bestowed,
   The many dire complaints
That sinners here on earth will make,
   With discontented saints,

About the doctors and their bills,
   The good and bad we did,
The lives our skill so often saved,
   Mistakes the earth had hid.

The strictures on our moral worth,
   The sins we do commit,
And universal dump we get,
   By wholesale in the pit.

For many hold 'twould be as hard
   Through Heaven's gate to wheedle
A doctor as to drive a camel through
   A hypodermic needle.

Yet in my dream there seemed to be
   Misapprehension here;
For I felt sure physicians will
   Among the saints appear.

A good old prophet told the Lord,
   Of Israel he alone
Remained His constant worshipper,
   All others bowed to stone.

This ancient saint was not the judge;
   Of neighbors he disdained
And in his zeal consigned to hell,
   God seven thousand claimed.

And may-be yet these "unco good,"
   Who think our chances slim,
May find the doctors climbing in
   To Heaven beside of them.

For from the fount from whence they're cleansed,
   E'en doctors may come clean;
God gives to no exclusive class
   The power to enter in.

And what there is beyond this life,
   There's nothing yet to seem.
We look to where death's curtain falls,
   And enter but to dream.

And thus I dreamt that round me stood
   The victims of disease,
The patients I had failed to cure,
   Though some had paid my fees.

One said, "It is a happy place,
   My bliss is unalloyed;
Through your mistakes just ten years more
   Of Heaven I have enjoyed.

"For if your treatment had been wise
   I still the earth would tread,
But thanks to your great want of skill
   I'm numbered with the dead."

Another made this queer complaint;
   "I'm prematurely sent;
The bungling doctors got me here
   Before development.

"I'm filled with love, my joy overflows,
   But what I most regret,
On earth I should have staid and got
   Capacity for it."

I here got shaky in my shoes,
   And asked if they'd attack us,
And raise a rumpus in these courts.
   With questions of malpractice.

"Oh, no! he said, "there's no redress,
   No righting this affliction:
For courts are not in session here
   For want of jurisdiction.

"And if there were, in our behalf
　We must ourselves appear;
A first-class lawyer can't be had,
　I never found one here.

At hearing this I felt composed,
　And wrapped my wings around me,
While dreamily with eyelids closed,
　Some other patients found me.

Here one with pleasant face appeared,
　Emotionally affected;
And soon another joined our group,
　Apparently dejected.

"Why," said the first, "I'm happy now
　As when I was forgiven,
And I have more to thank you for
　Than any one but Heaven.

"On earth, from infancy to age,
　I was afflicted there;
And would have prematurely died,
　But for your special care.

"Thanks to your skill, life was prolonged
　Till I was purged from sin,
And reached a soul development
　That takes all Heaven in!"

The one in disappointment found
　Found only in the seeming;
For recollect this is not Heaven,
　I'm only of it dreaming.

Burns had some thoughts, had they popped out
    Aught elsewhere but in bed,
Their sentiments no doubt had cost
    That pesky poet's head.

And if this clever-shallow dodge
    Political scribblers screen,
The church may pardon doctors who
    Heretically dream.

In justice to this one I'd make
    A just apology;
For souls, sometimes, are warped on earth
    By false theology.

She had been taught the Lord does take
    (And easily work it in)
A sinner's soul to make a saint's
    Impossible to sin.

And thus impressed she lived and died,
    And when my spirit fled,
To where it found her ghost up there,
    She was surprised and said:

"Why, doctor; how did you get here?
    I thought your morals brittle,
For at your patients you got mad,
    And sometimes swore a little.

"And is this just, my life was pure,
    And kept so till I died,
While you, so wicked there, have here
    As good a place supplied?"

My answer was, "When God made men,
    He made them to be brothers;
Repentant, then with pardon He
    Saved me as He saved others."

Just then another one appeared
    In robes of purest white,
Whose countenance was all aglow
    With rapturous delight.

I asked him, "Are you happy, sir?"
    His answer was expressed,
"It could not be, not to be,
    In company with the blest.

"I'm always happy, was on earth
    As soul on earth could be;
For man and heaven there are two parts
    And for our part you see,

"It's but to do as we are bid,
    Get down to our own biz,
And leaving others do the same,
    God will attend to His.

"I never thought in heaven's accounts
    I must arrange the rolls,
Or show God how to unwind the twist
    In others' cranky souls.

"And now I would not spoil the joy
    Of this bright blest abode
By setting up my judgment here,
    Upon the throne of God.

"Whom we find here Christ must have saved.
  Deny it as we might
On earth, up here in heaven we know
  Whatever is, is right."

Just then, on wings of starry gold,
  O'er crystal stream an angel swoops;
And all along its shining shore
  Came many more in happy groups.

And soon I felt the wing-fanned breeze,
  In balmy waves my forehead cool;
Magnolian sweets then filled the air,
  Wafted from o'er the burnished pool.

For all along that nether shore,
  Embowered 'mong trees of living green,
Were banks of buds of rare perfume,
  With brilliant flowering vines between;

And o'er its dimpled margin hung
  Rich clustering fruits of rarest hue;
Where myriad warbling songsters brought
  The birds of paradise to view.

And now I felt the angel's touch,
  I looked, and lo ! before me stood
The pinioned messenger I'd seen
  On shining wings come o'er the flood.

He said, "I'm sent to welcome you
  To all the beauties of the skies;
This side that river is not heaven,
  It is its glorious paradise.

"Here fresh from earth, the unfettered soul
  Expanding breathes the ambient air;
May bring from earth, but soon to lose,
  Impressions false engendered there.

"Now look beyond that placid stream,
  To yonder grove on mountain side,
Whose towering trees o'erspread the plain,
  And shade the verdant meadows wide.

"Those trees bear leaves the nations heal,
  Their eucalyptic branches are
More potent than cinchonic drugs,
  Or lactic sugar's mystic power.

"Go, pluck and eat, and soon forget
  All earth-born differences; made free
From all that's evil, you may dwell
  In blissful rest eternally."

I spread my wings to joyous flight,
  To pass beyond the pearly stream;
I wakened, and I found, alas,
  A ruptured bubble—'twas a dream.
                  —*Columbus Medical Journal.*

## ADDRESS TO THE MUMMY IN BELZONI'S EXHIBITION.

### BY HORACE SMITH.

And thou hast walked about (how strange a story!)
  In Thebes's streets three thousand years ago,
When the Memnonium was in all its glory,

And time had not begun to overthrow
These temples, palaces, and piles stupendous,
Of which the very ruins are tremendous!

Speak! for thou long enough hast acted dummy;
   Thou hast a tongue, come, let us hear its tune;
Thou'rt standing on thy legs above ground, mummy!
   Revisiting the glimpses of the moon.
Not like thin ghosts or disembodied creatures,
But with thy bones and flesh, and limbs and features.

Tell us—for doubtless thou canst recollect—
   To whom should we assign the Sphinx's fame?
Was Cheops or Cephrenez architect
   Of either pyramid that bears his name?
Is Pompey's pillar really a misnomer?
Had Thebes a hundred gates as sung by Homer?

Perhaps thou wert a mason, and forbidden
   By oath to tell the secrets of thy trade—
Then say, what secret melody was hidden
   In Memnon's statue, which at sunrise played?
Perhaps thou wert a priest. If so, my struggles
Are vain, for priestcraft never owned its juggles.

Perchance that very hand now pinioned flat,
   Has hob-a-nobbed with Pharoah, glass to glass;
Or dropped a half-penny in Homer's hat,
   Or doffed thine own to let Queen Dido pass,
Or held by Solomon's own invitation
A torch at the great temples' dedication.

I need not ask thee if that hand, when armed,
　　Has any Roman soldier mauled and knuckled,
For thou wert dead and buried and embalmed,
　　Ere Romulus and Remus had been suckled;
Antiquity appears to have begun
Long after thy primeval race was run.

Thou couldst develop, if that withered tongue
　　Might tell us what those sightless orbs have seen,
How the world looked when it was fresh and young,
　　And the great deluge had left it green;
Or was it then so old, that history's pages
Contained no record of its early ages?

Still silent, uncommunicative elf!
　　Art sworn to secrecy? Then keep thy vows;
But prithee tells us something of thyself;
　　Reveal the secrets of thy prison-house;
Since in the world of spirits thou hast slumbered,
What hast thou seen—what strange adventures numbered?

Since first thy form was in this box extended,
　　We have above ground, seen some strange mutations;
The Roman empire has begun and ended,
　　New worlds have risen—we have lost old nations,
And countless kings have into dust been humbled,
Whilst not a fragment of thy flesh has crumbled.

Didst thou not hear the pother o'er thy head,
　　When the great Persian conqueror, Cambyses,
Marched armies o'er thy tomb with thundering tread,
　　O'erthrew Osiris, Orus, Apis, Isis,
And shook the pyramids with fear and wonder,
When the gigantic Memnon fell asunder?

If the tomb's secrets may not be confessed,
   The nature of thy private life unfold,
A heart has throbbed beneath that leathern breast,
   And tears adown that dusky cheek have rolled;
Have children climbed those knees, and kissed that face?
What was thy name and station, age and race?

Statue of flesh, immortal of the dead!
   Imperishable type of evanescence!
Post-humous man, who quittest thy narrow bed,
   And standest undecayed within our presence,
Thou wilt hear nothing till the judgment morning;
When the great trumps shall thrill thee with its warning.

Why should this worthless tegument endure,
   If its undying guest be lost forever?
O, let us keep the soul embalmed and pure,
   In living virtue that when both must sever,
Although corruption may our frame consume,
The immortal spirit in the skies may bloom.

---

## THE CHILD'S ORIGIN.

"Our friend, David Baker, Esq.," says an Eastern paper, "who has produced some of the best poetry ever written by a Maine bard, pleased at a little incident that happened to his family, the first occurrence of the kind, gives vent to his feelings in the following imaginative piece:

### MY CHILD'S ORIGIN.

One night as old St. Peter slept,
   He left the door of Heaven ajar,
When through a little angel crept
   And came down with a falling star.

One summer as the blessed beams
 Of morn approached, my blushing bride
Awakened from some pleasing dreams,
 And found that angel by her side.

God grant but this—I ask no more,
 That when he leaves this world of pain
He'll wing his way to that bright shore,
 And find his way to Heaven again.


Whereupon some fellow of the practical sort, and without any imagination, and not possessing the "Divine Afflatus," attempts to destroy the little illusion of David, as follows:

### ST. PETER'S REPLY.

Full eighteen hundred years or more,
 I've kept my gate securely tyled
There was no "little angel" strayed,
 Nor one been missing all the while.

I did not sleep, as you supposed,
 Nor left the gate of Heaven ajar,
Nor has " a little angel " left,
 And gone down with a falling star.

Go ask that " blushing bride," and see
 If she don't frankly own and say
That when she found that angel babe,
 She found it in the good old way.

God grant but this—I ask no more—
 That should your number still enlarge
You'll not do as you did before,
 And lay it to old Peter's charge.

www.ingramcontent.com/pod-product-compliance
Lightning Source LLC
Chambersburg PA
CBHW020113030726
47498CB00006B/2078